A
Bachelor Party
for
Odysseus

A Bachelor Party for Odysseus

A Novel

Albert M. Balesh

SUNSTONE
PRESS

SANTA FE

Sunstone books may be purchased for educational, business, or sales promotional use.
For information please write: Special Markets Department, Sunstone Press,
P.O. Box 2321, Santa Fe, New Mexico 87504-2321.
Cover art by Ofelia Molinar
Book and cover design › Vicki Ahl
Body typeface › Benjamin
Printed on acid-free paper
∞
eBook 978-1-61139-390-3

Library of Congress Cataloging-in-Publication Data

Balesh, Albert M., 1952-
  A bachelor party for Odysseus : a novel / by Albert M. Balesh.
    pages cm
  ISBN 978-1-63293-074-3 (softcover : alk. paper)
  I. Title.
  PS3602.A59546B33 2015
  813'.6--dc23

                              2015022956

WWW.SUNSTONEPRESS.COM
SUNSTONE PRESS / POST OFFICE BOX 2321 / SANTA FE, NM 87504-2321 /USA
(505) 988-4418 / ORDERS ONLY (800) 243-5644 / FAX (505) 988-1025

Sunstone Press is committed to minimizing our environmental impact on the planet. The paper used in this book is from
responsibly managed forests. Our printer has received Chain of Custody (CoC) certification from: The Forest Stewardship Council™
(FSC®), Programme for the Endorsement of Forest Certification™ (PEFC™), and The Sustainable Forestry Initiative® (SFI®).

The FSC® Council is a non-profit organization, promoting the environmentally appropriate, socially beneficial and economically
viable management of the world's forests. FSC® certification is recognized internationally as a rigorous environmental and social
standard for responsible forest management.

Dedication

For Mom and Dad.
You did your best to raise seven children, and
"failed" with me. No one is perfect.

Contents

1

Long Haul's End

It was not always this way. That is, unless he had awakened from a long winter's sleep, and all was a dream. At one time, he had, had the world by the balls. Tall, handsome, well-spoken, sharp of wit, all the essentials to make a go of it. A natural born leader. A great catch. Yes, young Alex Bales had lacked nothing.

But the years had passed so quickly, and with them the joy of life itself. There was a time when even the simplest of pleasures had served as a safety valve to the pressures of a stressed-out existence. A good book, a new record, a night at the movies; all had provided psychotherapy, a drugless cure to the ailment that success had wrought.

Not that Alex was not grateful. He prayed everyday, thanking God for his position in life. After all, stress was just an occupational hazard; something that went with the turf. It sure beat panhandling, or calorie-counting at a Salvation Army or halfway house. Alex couldn't complain. Things could be much worse.

Something was missing, however. Something he could not buy. As he carefully examined the wrinkled skin of his hands and the varicose veins of his once well-sculpted legs, he became painfully aware of the fact that mortality was an awful adversary. His friends often called him vain. They would say that if ever a man could cheat death itself, it would be Alex himself to do the deed. But the fountain of youth, like Templar gold, exists more in the realm of REM sleep than in the universe of solids, liquids, and gases.

As a man grows older, he contents himself with his ever-faithful companion, with his memories, and with his grandchildren. Not Alex. Two divorces in his youth had left him childless and barren in the fertile terrain of love. Sure, he'd had many mistresses in his time, and was still more than a match for Viagra, but the waning of the spark of love was now starting to take its toll on him.

Depression is a funny thing. It often takes the form of a truth denied, until the victim is regurgitated from its viselike jaws. Alex had failed to come to terms with his depressive state for over thirty years. The next day was always going to be better. Then, 10,950 days later, a stark realization had set in. The inkblot on his mental health might, indeed, be indelible. What to do? Who to turn to? Those were the major existential questions of Alex Bales' life.

It was much too late to reconstruct burnt bridges. The few friends Alex possessed attributed his melancholia to male menopause, or to a CEO's change-of-life. Dark clouds would certainly pass. After all, money could buy anything, and Alex Bales was far from being a poor man. Business acquaintances advised long vacations, rich men's toys, and flings with beautiful, young women. All Alex could think about, however, was a proverbial pact with the devil. Faust would have found a more than suitable drinking companion in his company.

Then there was Randy Danhurst, Alex's best friend. A washed-out attorney and Harvard Law graduate, with his heart in the right place, Randy had never really assumed his rightful place in the Bar. So, he had taken up permanent residence at the bar. All forms of drinking and drugs had become Larry and Curly, fitting companions to his Moe, in life's comedy of errors.

Alex had felt pity for Randy, a being more mentally destitute than himself, and had gladly and willingly hired him to handle legal matters in his medical supply corporation. It was no great matter that Randy had been skimming off the top for many years now. Drugs had been an expensive commodity, and Alex knew that he was not evil at heart. What counted more than all else was Randy's accessibility. When Alex sent a distress signal, his friend was always there to heed the S.O.S.

They often spent Friday evenings in each other's company. After all, those long, cold Chicago winters could bore the hell out of a man, if there were not someone to inject some warmth into an otherwise frigid situation.

Alex and Randy often shared the same cigars, the same drinks, and the same women. Brotherhood meant much more to them than a mere slash at the palm and an exchange of some corpuscles.

One evening, while seated at the bar in one of their favorite Ontario Street haunts, Alex turned to Randy and said, "You know, I'd give it all up for thirty more good years."

"What are you talking about?" his friend replied absentmindedly, his gaze turned to the green olive in his martini, which he was trying to spear with a plastic party toothpick.

"I mean it, Randy, I'd give it all up to go back in time. All the money, all the pussy, all the success."

"How much have you had to drink?"

"It's not that, Randy," Alex slurred. "I'm just sick of everything. Look at me. My double chin casts a shadow, and I can barely get it up any more."

Randy did not know whether to empathize or laugh out loud. Alex was a moody character, and the more you took him seriously, the more he could drag you both down. Randy chose the middle ground. He turned to Alex, after giving up on the elusive olive, and said, "C'mon, Al, let's talk to those two blondes in the black miniskirts over there."

Randy's magic bullet appeared to do the trick, at least for the time being. The thrill of the hunt momentarily supplanted tears in one's beer. The night was still young. There would be time enough, later on in the evening at last call, to feel sorry for oneself.

The Loop Club was the kind of meat market that Chicago's nouveau riche and most influential players had come to call home. Their homes away from home. It served as both a watering hole and a mental health institution. Depending on the circumstances, it was a rendezvous point, a boardroom, and a place where pinstripe suits and blue jeans and cowboy boots mixed as well as black, white, and brown in an integrated neighborhood. Many a Polish maid and Cuban refugee had found immigration papers in the bowels of its inner sanctum, couched living room, and upstairs' coat closets. That the Loop Club was Mafia-owned and run was of little consequence to local politicians, physicians, and Chicago's finest, who sought sexual release, boasting rights, and social redemption in the mouth of some fair-haired beauty.

As Alex and Randy approached their unsuspecting prey, Alex noticed something was not right. Almost like an out-of-body experience, he observed the entire scene from high above. He saw Randy touch the shoulder of one of the young women, who did not seem to mind, and he even heard himself recite that famous rap that in the past had garnered him more than a few bed companions on cold winter's nights.

It was as if Alex's senses had suddenly become more attuned to his immediate environment. He could now see things much better, whispers were amplified, and touch had the subtlety of a sledgehammer. When Isabella, the taller of the two women, said that she would like another Cosmopolitan, her long and covetous glance at his gold money clip was not lost on him.

Painful clarity was his. Why had he not seen it sooner? Without even the formality of a good-bye, he distanced himself from the party of three. Randy, who was hot in pursuit of corporeal pleasures, took no notice of Alex's departure.

As he sought solace on a barstool at the far end of the dance floor, Alex gazed into his Jack Daniels on the rocks. He stirred it, like some witch's brew. Now that the truth had become evident to him, he hoped that the potion that lay before him would provide the solutions he so desperately needed. His train of thought, however, was suddenly interrupted by the arrival of old Randy.

"Where the hell did you go?"

"I can't take it, Randy. I can't take this anymore."

"What?"

"You heard me, old friend. What are we doing with our lives? You and I aren't worth a shit."

Randy realized, at that point, that the cure for what ailed Alex would not be found in a casual amplexus or a short trip to the coatroom upstairs. No, this time it was different. The bags under Alex's eyes, and the wrinkles and frown of his mouth, convinced Randy that his buddy's case just might be terminal. But what to do? He was not qualified to carry the ball for his friend. The long years of substance abuse had not only perfected his tremor, but increased his reputation as a fumbler. He was no good for himself, let alone for anyone else.

What was Alex thinking? As he looked over at Randy, no more than two feet away, he thought, "What a worthless individual." A thought, just a thought, that he would never utter to his friend.

"You know, Randy, I wish I were younger. I'd change everything."

"What brought this on, Alex?"

"What kinds of lives are we leading? We're going nowhere."

"Forget it," Randy slurred, his head now too heavy with drink to hold it up erect. "I know where you're going with this. Just forget it."

"I can't. Did you see Isabella? She could have cared less about me. It's the green, Randy. That's all she, and they, care about."

"Get real, Alex, or were you looking for a long, meaningful relationship?" The playfulness in Randy's voice was misinterpreted as sarcasm by Alex, and served to irritate him all the more.

"You just don't understand. Then, again, how could you. Your head is so full of drugs that only a brain transplant could get you to see things clearly."

With that, Randy got up abruptly and left. At that moment, Alex felt extremely sorry for what he had said. Oh, well, Randy would get over it. He always did. Besides, there were problems much graver than his. Alex knew that his whole life and his utter existence now hung in the balance. So, he was not about to concern himself with hurt feelings, painful nerve endings, or personality clashes.

The present situation required serious thought, and, perhaps, a dash of coffee. In the wee hours of the night in that bar on Ontario Street, as he watched the patrons slowly file out and began to infuse caffeine, Alex resolved to change his life. The destination was evident. The road to be traveled, however, still had to be decided upon. That would not be easy.

Alex's life flashed through his mind; the successes and the failures. He had come from a very wealthy and influential Chicago family, and had graduated at the top of his class from Northwestern University School of Business. Twice married to beautiful and well-placed women, neither of whom had provided him with an heir, although both had been more than willing and able, he had absorbed himself in his work to cover the hurt of their loss and the financial burden imposed by regular alimony payments. His successes in the professional arena had for a time even erased the memories of a failed personal life, as he graced the cover of Business Week and rose to become the youngest chairman and CEO of a multinational, multibillion dollar corporation. All this had given him some semblance of happiness. I think, therefore I am. Success in business had been transduced into tranquility on the mental playing field.

What was missing now? Where was the missing link? Money he had, and fame to boot. Then why was he not happy? At 60 years old, he still cut an impressive figure, although ambient lighting now made up a greater proportion of the key and essential ingredients composing his persona.

Alex thought about this, and more, for what seemed like hours. A glance at his wristwatch, however, served as a reality check. He had been seated there at the bar for an eternity of fifteen minutes. While that was more than enough time to have reached most of the corporate decisions he had made in his lifetime, it was far too little to pacify a soul in torment.

Just then, it came to him; the common denominator. What do you give the man who has everything? Not an easy question to answer, and yet it was right in front of him all the time. As the clock struck four a.m., and as the last of the stragglers clumsily stumbled out of the Loop Club into the cold morning air, a glimmer of a smile erased the signs of age at the corners of Alex's mouth. He had done it. The solution was well within reach. Why had he not thought of it sooner? So smart, and yet he was so dumb.

As the bartender intoned his last call and a drunken, dishwater blonde attempted to seat herself on the barstool next to him, Alex could not have been happier. Those distractions were minor, for he had found the Holy Grail. He could not wait to tell his friend Randy. He would tell him immediately. Yes, the world was a glorious place, after all.

Alex could not refrain from giving Susie, the dishwater blonde, a great big kiss on the cheek. After buying her a last round and giving the bartender a twenty dollar tip, he extricated himself from the Loop Club's womb. Then, he thought better. Why should he have looked a gift horse in the mouth. Maybe the night was still young, after all, and all that was needed was a jumpstart to check out the "horse" more closely. A young man, he was not, but he would be more than a match for this inebriated hussy. So, putting himself into reverse, he reentered the Loop Club and made for the point of no-return, where he had left Susie in a holding pattern.

"So, you came back," was her not unexpected initial foray into the small-talk arena.

"I couldn't live without you."

"Aw, c'mon. We're too old for that."

"Speak for yourself," was Alex's not-so-witty retort.

"Where do we go from here?"

"Well, I'd usually say 'My place or yours?' but it's gotta be yours."

"Why's that?"

"Because I never return to the scene of the crime, namely, my place, which happens to be a mess right now. So, I'm not receiving any visitors. By the way, did I get your name?"

"My name is Susan, Suzanne, or Susie, depending on my mood. Tonight I'm Susie, but I'll answer to anything you call me, as long as you're gentle."

"Okay, Susie."

As they left the club together, and mounted his trusty steed, a Porsche 911, all Alex could think about was how much he had left in his proverbial "tank." Testicles and testosterone levels were always a concern in his physiological garage. He himself was no longer a performance vehicle, and he knew he'd have to squeeze every last drop through his "carburetor," in order to get his sexual mileage of old.

"Where to, Susie?"

"I live on North Milwaukee Avenue, Six Thousand North."

So, in a roar of the engine and his man-juices, they were off. The cramped quarters of the vehicle did nothing for his rheumatism, but did aid placement of her left hand on his "jewels." As his "sleeping lion," as he used to refer to his penis, began to come to life, he pointed his two-seated chariot in the direction of his willing prey's domicile; the image in his mind of what was to transpire and the motor's hum made his osseous rattles more bearable. As he dug his spurs into the accelerator and pointed towards Susie's lair, he became flustered with excitement, and began to perspire profusely.

Her apartment was simple enough. Nothing extravagant. Just the bare essentials necessary for a single, working girl who had seen better days and happier times; when a loving husband and several small, happy, and obedient children had constituted the sum-total of her universe. A drinking problem, wandering hands and eyes, and a fear of growing old and unattractive had sent her life into a tailspin. Divorce, child custody, and failed rehab had been a logical follow-up, which she had buried in the attorneys' files, if not in her mind's closet, twenty years before. In short, she was a wreck, and Alex was not adverse to plundering her.

"So, what's your name?"

"I used to be called Alex."

"Used to be?"

"Tonight I prefer 'Willis,' but you can call me 'Will;' and, I hope I don't offend you when I say that all I want to hear from you is 'I will.'"

That was that. Alex had no idea how Susie would react to that affirmation, but it was four forty-five a.m. now, and he wanted to get the job done before the morning sun arose.

"Don't worry, Will, Alex, or whatever you want me to call you. I'm not looking to go steady, and I certainly don't want your pity. Maybe we can help each other out. If you'll hold me in your arms, and just let me pretend for a half-hour or so, I'll do anything you ask; and I mean anything."

Alex reacted to that declaration with a puzzled look, which was not lost on Susie.

"What's wrong?"

For the life of himself, he could not answer. She had not only taken him by surprise, but she had made her eventual conquest too easy. Even a sixty-year-old doesn't want it handed to him on a silver platter. Oh, what the heck. Time was "a-wastin," and he had to get this over with; not only to reinforce his sexual prowess, but also to get back on the road and over to Randy's place. It was not that he wished to apologize to his friend, it was only that he would take great pleasure in detailing the "blow-by-blow," both literally and figuratively, to his best friend.

Without further formality or ticking of the minute hand, he grabbed Susie by the waist, buried his lips into her neck, and moved her not-so-gently over to the living room sofa, upon which he and she fell. As he clumsily went for the zipper and buttons of her short skirt, he resembled more of an "all thumbs" cub scout than the debonair lover he had once aspired to be and, in some circles, actually attained. He heard a slight rip, as Susie's skirt came apart, and, before good sense and chivalry could win the day, he found his nose and lips buried in a bush whose odor was a combination of a female hygiene deodorant and cat sweat; which most likely emanated from the sofa on which the festivities would last for a mere thirty minutes or so, although they seemed like hours.

When Alex came to, he soon came to realize that while his pants were gone, his socks, shoes, and dress shirt were still glued to his body. To make matters worse, when he tried to recall what had transpired in their last half-hour, all was a blur and a myriad of images with no unifying theme to speak of. Susie was sprawled out on the sofa, fast asleep, with one leg on the sofa itself and the other dangling in midair between sofa and floor. As he got off of her and made a beeline in the dark for what he thought was the bathroom, he ended up in the kitchen. Rather than play Robinson Crusoe in the dark, he let fly with a long overdue piss in the kitchen sink, washed his hands with sink-top Ajax powdered cleanser, and made for the living room again. Slipping into his pants and not observing a stir from Susie, he stole a quick glance at his wristwatch. It was five twenty a.m. He must get over to Randy's now, not to vaunt his sexual acrobatics, which, frankly, he could not remember, but to try to make peace.

Alex was not proud of himself as he took one last look back at Susie, placed two new, crisp one hundred dollar bills on the sofa next to her, and evacuated the scene of his "conquest." As he pointed his four-wheeled steed toward Lake Shore Drive, he became flustered with excitement and began to perspire profusely. He had so much to tell Randy, and there was nothing he could do to calm the waters and buttress the banks of his mind against the onslaught of thoughts.

His orderly train of cerebration, though not derailed, was well on the track to schizophrenia. That must not occur, however. Rumination might be dissociated, but mission was assuredly clear. Racing down Lake Shore Drive to the tempo of Lake Michigan's waves crashing on the shoreline, Alex became empowered with both hindsight and foresight. This newfound ability to see all and do all would inject meaning into his life from that moment on. No more idle chatter. No more wasted days and nights. No more waking up in strange places with his stockings on and an unfamiliar bedfellow next to him, after what had just occurred that night. All that was over, although he had sworn that before. What he most needed now was a strategist or a counselor to draw up plans and lay down the groundwork for his spiritual coup d'etat. That was where Randy would fit in.

The twenty-minute drag race from North Milwaukee Avenue and down Lake Shore Drive ended on North Sheridan Road, where Randy's condominium was located. Alex's heart palpitated wildly in anticipation of his forthcoming revelations to his friend. He greeted the doorman, who agreed to bed down his mare, and was told that Randy had entered the premises alone about three hours before. A futile attempt to ring him up from the lobby led Alex to become proactive. It was now almost daylight.

What happened next was more crepuscular than real, like living a dream or watching a silent movie in slow motion. Denial and conversion reaction are unfettered beasts. As Alex boarded the elevator for a rapid ascent to the sixteenth floor, time froze and lock-down was instantaneous. In what seemed eerily like the splitting of a second or the blink of an eye, he found himself standing in front of Randy's door.

Something was wrong. Something just did not add up. What was it? Where was this going? It did not take long for Alex to observe that the door had been left ajar. Silence. No response to his entreaties. As Alex burst through the door across the threshold, nothing could have prepared him for the sight he was about to fall witness to. There, spread-eagle and dorsal on the living room floor, about six feet from the door, lay Randy. He was stark naked, and his skin shown ashen white. Eyes flared open and mouth agape, Randy had been preserved for eternity in that sculpted gesture of primordial scream, which had never come. His right hand had formed a fist that lay over his left hemithorax. White powder had dusted his upper lip, nostrils, and chin, and the oriental carpet in the middle of the living room showed traces of the same substance.

One did not have to be a mathematician to put two and two together. Mother Cocaine had burned another prodigal son. Alex was at once overcome by an overpowering urge to vomit. He left his friend there, and, in an attempt to gain the bathroom toilet, succeeded only in reaching the bathtub.

Flashing lights, muffled voices, fingers in the eyes. Loss of consciousness provided only a momentary respite from the grim reality of just minutes before. When Alex finally regained his senses, he looked past the two paramedics, who knelt over him, to the bathroom doorway. He almost expected to see Randy standing there, a look of relief on his wrinkled face and an "I told you so" in his eyes. That was not to be, however, as chills from his mind's cold shower replaced the status quo of his imagination.

One of the paramedics, an older man of robust build, gently told Alex to lie there quietly until they could check him out thoroughly. "Just stay calm, and we'll be through in a moment," should have reassured Alex and convinced him of the ordinariness of the situation. It had the completely opposite effect, as his friend's demise and the appearance on the scene of the EMTs had been as totally unexpected and unprepared for as a kick to the balls.

He began to struggle wildly, and screamed to see his friend Randy. An inadvertent punch was thrown at the second paramedic, who took the blow without batting an eye, as if to say, "I understand. I'd probably do the same thing in your shoes." And just as Alex's fury reached a crescendo, the tall, gaunt figure of a Chicago homicide inspector, Detective Joe Marbry, appeared from who knew where. He must have been there the entire time, casing Dr. Jekyll, while hoping to catch a glimpse of Mr. Hyde.

"Are you feeling better, Mr. Bales?"

"How do you know my name?" Alex responded instinctively to the detective's query.

"Please forgive me. My name is Detective Marbry, and I went through your wallet. Standard procedure in cases like this."

"Cases?"

"Suspected homicides."

"What are you talking about, Marbry? Even an ass can see that Randy committed suicide. Don't ask me why, though. If anything, I should be out there, and he should be in here right now, sharing tea and crumpets with the likes of you."

At that last remark, what appeared to be a smirk deepened the right angle of Detective Marbry's mouth. The unexpected black humor and awkwardness of situations like this took some getting used to. Twenty years on the force had not been sufficient to immunize the good inspector and camouflage the appearance of his oral companion.

"I know you're upset. Maybe we can do this some other time, or perhaps you wouldn't mind coming down to the precinct station with me right now. Sooner or later, though, I'm going to need a statement."

"Let's get this over with. Randy OD'd. He was a junkie, a lush, a lecher, and a pervert, by your standards, but he was my friend. My only friend. Sure, he was unhappy. Aren't we all? Sure, he had things to hide; those skeletons that rattle in all of our closets. But you and I are no better than he. Yes, we're alive, but I, for one, dread the dawn. And you, Detective Marbry, what does tomorrow hold for you? More unpleasantness, I'm sure. Two of us died out there in the living room. Randy, who can bear you no witness, and I, a soul laid bare by witnessing that which should never be. More, Marbry, I can't tell you."

A pat on the shoulder and an "I see" were Marbry's only reactions.

2

Chance Encounter

Three months passed from that cold October night. If one were to ask Alex where they had gone, he certainly would not have been able to respond. Adrift in a sea of loneliness with only the barest essentials, he cared not whether those burning eyes of his would ever catch sight of land again. He was torn apart inside, and shipwreck was neither an unpleasant option nor one to be feared, when possibility of homecoming was erased.

Alex hoped he would never see Detective Marbry again after that fateful night. It would be better that way. Alex had learned the hard way on more than one occasion, however, that nothing was certain in this world of the barely living when it came to booze, broads, and beliefs. He could not help but think that all the players in his life were simply transient entities. Here today, gone tomorrow. Nothing more, nothing less. They left absolutely no impact on his life. After all, does one remember the bite of a mosquito when the swelling goes down?

Randy had been different, however. He had been as close as one could get to being his friend. Frankly, with the way Alex's existence had heretofore proceeded, that was saying a lot. And now, what to do. Too old to make new friends, too young to die, and a little too late to start over. It was no wonder that the last few months had not been easy.

They could not possibly have been. There was just too much psychological baggage to sort out, and the brain's conveyor belt had been temporarily out of order.

Alex knew that sooner or later he would pull through, but the task at hand was not an envious one. Future roads in his life promised to have so many forks that the road less traveled would be just as sure as the main thoroughfare. And although armies of psychologists, psychiatrists, social workers, and sociologists might be able to glue the pieces back together, placing Alex back on top of the wall would take far more than a sturdy ladder or a broad pair of shoulders.

Nothing gave Alex satisfaction anymore. Sure, the simplest and most meaningful things in life are free, but whoever said that they had to be enjoyable. Does the schizophrenic patient in a mental institution derive pleasure from a sunrise, a sunset, a rainbow, or the singing of lovebirds? Could Alex ever truly ponder that question and come up with its answer? Certainly, the monotony of his current day-to-day existence had deleted all emotion and subjective thinking, and had left the hard drive of his animus free to assimilate all the worst habits, notions, and philosophic inclinations conceivable.

He cared not whether he lived or died, and he took to serious drinking. A razor became both an instrument of torture to him and a complete waste of time. There was no sense grooming himself, as there was no one to impress, no one to pal around with, no double dating, no whoring, and no meaningful relationships. At a distance, his beard gave him an air of distinction, which was inevitably erased by his wrinkled clothing at close quarters. Alex was lost, despondent, and, as the Italians put it, "a terra," on the ground. The salt in his wounds no longer burned; it had long ago caked. His next train station in the railroad of life could only be a pharmacy, a garage, or a cold-steel asp in his bedroom dresser drawer.

Alex had been down many times before. On each occasion, he had mustered enough force to bounce back. Would this be different? Was this most current incubus to be the end? Had his survivor's instinct finally been sapped? That very morning the answers to those questions would not be forthcoming, but a stay of execution would be granted.

Alex awoke on that wintry morning of January 19, 2014 at eleven fifteen. He had by now adopted the habit of never arising before eleven o'clock. What would be the point of doing otherwise? After all, he no longer went to work, having delegated all authority to a counterpart who not only stole from the company, but had also managed to bed every willing female in a management position. You had to give him credit, he sure knew how to mix business with pleasure, or was it pleasure with business. In any case, Alex believed that to be a small price to pay for the luxury of being able to sleep in and forgoing the responsibilities of the day.

Rising from bed, Alex shivered as his bare feet touched down on the carpet less, parquet floor. A curse left his mouth, as he suddenly realized that he had forgotten to adjust the thermostat the night before. Alcohol does that to a man. It makes you think you're burning up, as icicles seed your beard and dangle from your testicles. How many times had Alex sworn up and down that he would never go to bed drunk again. And if he did, he would certainly remember to turn up the heat. Oh, well. Too late now.

Showering not a factor and laundry backed up two weeks, Alex made fast work of choosing his wardrobe for the day from the heap thrown on the floor at the foot of the bed. A pair of jeans, a turtleneck sweater, brown penny loafers, and matching stockings that did not smell too badly were the obvious and only choices. Five minutes later, he was out the door and on his way to the newsstand downstairs. The only thing that gave him even a semblance of pleasure was that morning quest for the newspaper, his newspaper, the Chicago Tribune.

He greeted Sam, the 67-year-old proprietor of the newsstand, as he had done almost everyday for the last three months.

"The usual, Alex?"

"Why? Is there something new on the menu?"

"Well, if you can't take a joke, then fuck you!"

Although the gleam in Sam's eye should have given Alex the cue to that good-natured ribbing, it became painfully obvious that the desired effect had been lost on him. The pincushion of Alex's fragile psyche had already been pierced by one too many needles. Sam had hoped for an effect, some kind of effect, any kind of effect, even a voodoo doll type of effect. It was clear, though, that three months of utter anguish had raised the bar beyond grasp. Alex's threshold for laughter was now unreachable. He no longer had a sense of humor. Sam did not need a PhD to decipher that blank stare. As he sent his friend and customer home with paper and change in hand, he looked skyward momentarily, as if to say, "God, don't let me read about him in tomorrow's news."

The return home was uneventful for Alex. His front door, however, triggered a flashback. Hard to believe, but now even inanimate objects appeared to exert some measure of control over him. Stop! He shook it off. Upon entering his apartment, he regained what little composure he had left. The heat had kicked in, and he was instantly grateful for one of life's little pleasures. It's funny, Alex thought, how a good meal, a good night's sleep, and a good roll in the hay had all been supplanted in his instinctual hierarchy by something as corny and ordinary as a thermostat. Revelations like this were many, especially recently. Although they never ceased to amaze him and had increased exponentially since the passing of Randy, this latest batch was utter magic.

Horizons were broadening. His mind was expanding. Perhaps where others had failed, Alex would now be able to tap into that mother lode of cerebral function long known to exist, and yet just out of reach of mere mortals. Nothing comes without a price, however. Whether it was a pound of flesh or thirty pieces of silver, just one look at Alex's physiognomy was enough to convince even the staunchest of doubters that a heavy toll had already been exacted. Appearances did not deceive. Alex felt ancient.

Settling into his favorite armchair, a worn, brown-leather beauty purchased in happier times, Alex vied for the proper nestling position. His posterior fit snugly into the perfectly formed indentation of the lower cushion, a depression made all the more functionally comfortable by its near daily use over the past three months. It was quite funny, Alex thought, the way he felt like a mother hen perched in all her glory upon her oval treasures, whenever he was seated there. The fact was, his makeshift throne exuded a sense of both safety and protection. It had become for him a zone of solace in his world gone awry.

The newspaper was a thin one, composed of no more than four sections. After all, it was Tuesday, and what could have possibly occurred on Monday to fill those branded sheets of tabloid. Alex donned his wire rimmed reading glasses, the right eyepiece of which showing an obvious crack, which would sooner or later fracture in a most inopportune time. No need to repair the lens now, though. In the quotidian with no priorities or urgency, a trip to the optician was neither auspicious nor in the cards.

Alex glanced quickly at the front-page headline. It took no more than a cursory view of the world's troubles for him to jettison the news entirely. His personal philosophy in the ways of mass media and its presentation of the woes of Homo sapiens was a simple one. He could not be bothered with the trials and tribulations of a planet that had turned a cold shoulder to him a long time ago. Fallen economies, wars, pestilence, and drought were coin of the realm for the saviors of the world, not the losers. The business and sports sections soon followed brother news. Alex's five-minute attention span was waning faster than ever, when he found refuge in the lifeboat of the classified section.

Classifieds were a home away from home, and the only place in a newspaper where individuals more desperate and destitute than himself could be found. They were the humble abode of con artists, salesmen, new age religions, unwanted animals, jobs too good to be true, defective collectors' pieces, private investigators, and an occasional messiah. Alex loved the classifieds, which made him whole. They convinced him that even in his madness, there was still a ways to go before reaching the gutter of their depravity. Human refuse he was, but a spark or stimulus of some kind might possibly ignite the carbon, hydrogen, and methane of his being. He found comfort in the fact that the others listed in those pages upon pages of ads had long ago been processed and compacted, and that the spreading of their remains on fertile fields would not trigger a fruitful harvest.

As he skimmed the miscellaneous section of the classifieds panning for gold, Alex was unsure of what even he was looking for. The scattered ripples of the miscellaneous, however, often brought the highest returns. It did not take long for his normally hyperkinetic eye muscles to calm and become transfixed on a small ad embossed in black. With all hints of nystagmus gone and the muscles of his extremities tensed, he was ready to spring. His jaw dropped a centimeter, allowing the makings of a subtle and imminent smile to show through. This was too good to be true.

There on paper, at the touch of his fingertips, was the solution to all his problems and the answer to prayers and entreaties uttered in desperation twenty years ago, when he was still a religious man. Whoever said that the powers that be do not allow conversion of imploration into some kind of supernatural certificate of deposit, to be withdrawn by the holder many years later at maturity. A king's ransom of interest can appear on the horizon when the soul is at its neediest.

Some distant church belfry tolled twelve noon, as the world seemed to stop and Alex read, "Edward Stawson, M.D., Fountain of Youth – Aging Reversed, call for appointment (773) 481-1952."

Alex paused, rubbed his eyes, and read the advertisement again.

A trickle of sweat on his brow was the external manifestation of the ad's inner effect on him. He wanted to scream, but a sudden episode of apnea precluded that. His state of inward and outward agitation would not last long. Alex would not let it. As he composed himself, he reached the only rational decision that irrationality could permit. He would visit Dr. Stawson, but not just yet. Extraordinary circumstances demanded extraordinary thought, and he must think, painful as that might be.

Alex was what you might call a thinker. Pensive by nature, he had found ample time to ponder his plight during the physical and mental debacle of the last three months. Cognitive processes were no longer a luxury. They had become an imperative, as he contemplated a vaster world, much greater than the microcosm of wrinkled sheets and stale air of his static abode. A life grinding to a halt had been superimposed on his gray matter's "business as usual." While his mind was at times still vibrant and dynamic in both intent and execution, the wind had been knocked out of his soul.

His musings often turned from the sublime to the profane, and criticism far superseded construction. One of Alex's favorite foods for thought was the distant rumbling of the drums of war. Not only was he at war with himself, but also with every living thing around him. With a body ravaged and a mind given no quarter, he chuckled inappropriately at the realization that Armageddon would not be unleashed on a level playing field. Bias and inequalities had run rampant, and rules of engagement were now ratified in corporate boardrooms, as fates hung in the balance. Collective souls were now bartered for over croissants and executive breakfasts. Wow! What a thought. If not a Pulitzer, Alex's streams of consciousness were certainly worthy of honorable mention. In a world devoid of humanity, his penance or sentence, whichever you prefer, was to be a philosopher. Such would have made even Dante proud.

Over an hour had passed in what an outsider might construe as a complete waste of time and loss of touch with reality. To Alex, however, what appeared to the untrained eye as mere sparkings of neural tissue long dead and obviously resistant to all attempts at resuscitation was in reality a conflagration just waiting to burst forth. The match in a storage closet of the mind would soon become a towering inferno, which no fire department on earth could extinguish.

But now, what to do? The larger view had been deciphered, and concoction of a game plan must perforce follow. Alex knew that he must socialize that evening, not because he cherished company, but because revelations and burning bushes had always appeared to him in noisy environments. He slated a pilgrimage to his favorite spiritual Mecca on Ontario Street for that very evening. He was off to see the Wizard, and perhaps Chicago was not so far from Kansas after all.

The Loop Club had always been his refuge from mind storms. It had the flavor of an unobtrusive, neighborhood bar that had weathered the transition over the years from bathtub gin and numbers games to yuppie suavity and double-parked Porsches. Bill Jacobson and Bob Reynolds, the owners, had known Alex for years, and had seen him go from bad to worse. Neither, however, had ever sought to intervene or rescue. They could not, for each had too many problems of his own. Furthermore, unwritten rules dictated respect of staked-out territory, whether it be marked by urine or otherwise.

It was nine p.m., and as Alex crossed the threshold of the Loop Club's bulletproof front door, he was greeted by a chorus of two. Bill and Bob had seen him walk through the door almost simultaneously, and the raucousness of their voices was music to his ears. Their occasional barbs and goodhearted insults had been more precious to him, in the past, than even the most beautiful concerto by Mozart or aria sung by Maria Callas. On more than one occasion, Bill and Bob had been lifeboats to Alex in a proverbial sea of despair.

"Where the hell have you been?" intoned Bob.

"How's it hanging, Alex?" added Bill.

"Correction, Bill. It's hanged," blurted Bob, good-naturedly.

"You know, you guys can kiss my big, hairy ass. I just came in here for a drink, and that's the thanks I get. Your ugly pusses just happen to be part of the deal."

"Hmm, okay. We can take a hint. Good to see that you haven't changed a bit, Alex. That rosy disposition of yours will work wonders on the ladies," chided Bill.

"Who said anything about ladies? Can't a guy get a drink in here without you guys riding his ass. Honestly, guys. Just give me the usual, and I'll take my place in my niche in the back booth."

"The usual? What the hell is that?" Bob smirked.

"Okay. I'm leaving."

"Jesus, Alex. What's wrong with you? Bob, give him his Guinness, and leave him to his perversions in the back."

Armed with his elixir for thought, Alex slowly proceeded to the isolated haven of a back booth, far from the mayhem of Bill, Bob, the jukebox, and stray pheromones, testosterones, and estrogens. Instinctively, however, he did do a 360 degree, before reaching his final destination. Who could know? One actually never knew. Salvation might lie in the arms, in the mind, or between the legs of one hapless, soon-to-be-discovered member of the opposite sex. After convincing himself to the contrary, Alex hunkered down in his booth for a protracted skirmish with his inner demons and a one-man strategy session. A plan for the upcoming week would have to be formulated in every detail.

The ad he had read that morning in the *Chicago Tribune* had certainly been intriguing. C'mon, fountain of youth? Aging reversed? Who was that charlatan Dr. Stawson trying to fool? Alex was a grown man, a little down on his luck of late, but nonetheless a grown man. Throughout his life, wheeler-dealers had tried to pull countless fast ones over on him. It went with the turf. Nary a one, however, had ever succeeded. Now this quack, this poor excuse for a medical practitioner and man of science was going to have the balls to try again. Did he know with whom he was dealing?

For an hour Alex nursed his Guinness Stout and entertained a vast array of thoughts and impulses, some common to his fellow man and others unequivocally personal. He remembered a cold, Sunday morning fifty-one years in the past, when his favorite uncle had taken him as a boy to see a "Dracula" movie. His father's brother had meant no harm, nor could he have possibly conceived of the effect of that cinema outing on the boy's later life. Although the nightmares of that Sunday night, long ago, had long since ceased, the indelible scars on Alex's psyche had not been definitively buried with the Count. He had learned, however, how to cosmetically suppress them and fight back. When something he feared, like the vampires of his youth, challenged him in later life, he negated its existence with slight of hand and force of will.

Half a century had been more than enough time to hone those skills and make Alex the master of his fate. Depressed he was. No one could deny that. Fearful? Not a chance. Fearful of what? He feared no one and nothing. He had built a modest business empire and risen to the acme of his profession, aided by nothing other than a pure and simple disdain for all that others feared. There was no Achilles heel to be found. There was no chink in his armor. There were no telltale skeletons in his closet. His colleagues and employees had viewed him as a cross between Sir Lancelot and Jack the Ripper. He had been totally incorruptible morally, with go-for-the-throat professional instincts. That sum total had made Alex untouchable. Then Randy had died.

The walls had suddenly come tumbling down, and with them Alex's sense of his own mortality. Perhaps that had been it. Perhaps this had all boiled down to man's inherent, primordial fear of death, which had touched him by extrapolation.

A smile came to his face. He had now solved the riddle of the Sphinx. The only thing left for Alex to do now was to throw body and soul into gear and travel the one path available. That path would lead to a telephone call and a face-to-face encounter with a shady individual who would most likely promise to deliver that which Mother Nature, human physiology, or the grace of God had been heretofore unable to concede.

A sudden excitement came over him, as Alex shifted into fourth and manic. The GPS and cruise control for the rest of his life had been set, and he had only to pick a final destination. His mind's voyage, however, whether in the world of fantasy or reality, became temporarily sidetracked as a voice brought the roar of his engine and the roll of his tires to a screeching halt.

"Is anyone sitting there?"

Alex looked up, from the bosom of his booth, to see a slim, dishwater blonde peering into his privacy. The audacity. Was nothing sacred?

"What?" was the closest to a sentence that Alex could muster on such short notice.

"Is anyone sitting there?" came the query, again, as if only milliseconds had ensued, and the reverberations had returned by ricochet off one of the four walls.

"No. Have a seat."

"Hi. My name is Judy, and I saw you sitting there all alone. Actually, Bob and Bill sent me over. They thought you could use the company."

As Alex gazed into the green eyes of the somewhat attractive invasion of his turf, he was struck by the notion that Thomas Edison, Alexander Graham Bell, Louis Pasteur, and perhaps even Albert Einstein had all most likely been caught up in similar circumstances. To be on the verge of startling and awe-inspiring discoveries, only to be brought down to earth by a chance meeting, some small talk, a bill to be paid, a baby's cries, or a knock at the door was par for the course. Such was the fate of great men, Alex concluded. Metal tempered by the banal and the profane was no less lustrous, only more unwieldy.

"Look, Judy," Alex could feel his lips moving like a runaway train, "I'm sure you're a wonderful person, but school's out and Social Security is on the way."

"Who said anything about long-lasting relationships, and I didn't get your name," Judy snapped. After all, alone she was, but Florence Nightingale she was not.

"Alex, but you can call me 'Dad,'" came the inevitable retort of the inmate who had just cleared the invisible barbwire, and was making a beeline for the front door with his soon-to-be conquest.

Upon negotiation of the last obstacle in his path, a drooling drunk, with Judy in tow, Alex did not forget to salute his two friends, Bill and Bob, as he pierced the night air and its promise of freedom. He turned, flipped them the bird, and was gone with his "fool's gold."

3

Make Me an Offer

The next day began just like the previous one hundred and eighty, but with one small difference. The new day's small glimmer of hope might indeed transform itself into a conflagration of salvation. Alex awoke for the first time, in God knows how long, with a positive attitude. He had even engineered a coup of some kind by eclipsing his usual wakeup time of eleven a.m. by five full hours. As he took a seat in front of long-lost companions, "Snap, Crackle, and Pop," he came to realize that breakfast was one of life's little pleasures that he had long ago forgone. An early morning stomach full of whole grains, rice, and other solids was certainly preferable to the ethanol diet he had come to subsist on. Today, for all practical purposes, a celebration was in order. In a little over three hours, Alex would be making the telephone call that would change his life. At least, he was highly hopeful that would be the case. Should it not be, things could not get any worse. Then the order of business would be to clean the Beretta pistol, which lay on top of his underwear in the bedroom dresser drawer. Placement of the firearm in that particular location had been a crucial detail. Were it to be necessary to be rushed to a hospital emergency room for any reason, he would not be caught dead without clean underwear. Alex chuckled, as he thought, perhaps he had missed the boat. Underwear would have absolutely no significance at that point, and rumination was now better directed elsewhere.

As distant church bells tolled nine a.m., Alex felt an involuntary spasm of his right thigh muscle. He was being propelled into a vertical position. He knew what would come next. As he slowly but surely closed the distance between himself and Alexander Graham Bell's legacy, he felt the calm that only confession and absolution can bring. After the telephone call that he was about to make, he would be ready for death if the voice on the other end of the line did not extend a fig leaf or a promise of hope. Alex was ready. The sun shone brightly. The buzz of the city foreshadowed future life, and perhaps even future shock, as he dialed (773) 481-1952.

It did not take long, two rings to be exact, for a female voice to answer on the other end.

"Hello."

"Hello. I'd like to make an appointment to see Dr. Stawson, please."

"May I have your name, please?"

There was something quite irritating about the receptionist's voice. Although Alex could not put his finger on what it was, he knew the voice to be a cross between that of a Jewish American Princess and a female Count Dracula. Her diction was perfect. Her patience most likely was not.

"The doctor doesn't know me. I saw his recent ad in the *Chicago Tribune*, and I'd like to make an appointment."

"May I have your name, please?" this time her voice emitting a tone of militant dominance.

Alex, however, appeared incapable of answering that simple question. Either all was too good to be true, or he thought that by uttering his name, he might be turning the key in a door he was not ready to open.

"I just told you. The doctor doesn't know me. Now, if you'll be kind enough to tell me when I can see him, I'll go on with my life and let you go on with yours."

Alex was getting flustered, although the root of his aggravation was a mystery even to himself. After all, this minimum-wage gatekeeper had asked but a simple question. One step closer to hanging up, he momentarily pondered what it was going to take to complete the mission and make the appointment. Resolve was not an issue here. Alex's civility, on the other hand, was about to become one.

"Why do you want to make an appointment?" the receptionist chimed in, now matter-of-factly.

Alex was about to tell her to kiss his ass and forget the whole thing, when a startling revelation came to mind. This woman could have cared less whether he made an appointment or not, and yet her immediate importance in the balance of the rest of his life could not be underestimated. She held the key to the crypt, and it would be through her mediation that he would be armed with crucifix and all manner of charms and amulets to vanquish his demons. As analogies raced through his mind, Alex settled upon a circus of life motif. He was the tightrope walker, the star of the show. She was but a hired hand, a creature delegated to maintain the safety net below. Hers was not the glory, but the power. It was imperative that he now become convinced of this, or all was lost. Alex decided to play along.

"Actually, I want to see Dr. Stawson about his 'fountain of youth' project. I think it might help me, and I'd like to see the doctor as soon as possible."

"All right. Will ten o'clock tomorrow morning be okay, Mister...?"

"Bales. Alex Bales."

"Ten o'clock tomorrow, Mr. Bales?" the receptionist repeated again, matter-of-factly.

"Okay. That'll be fine."

"See you tomorrow."

Alex could sense that she was about to hang up.

"Hold it." he growled involuntarily. "Where are you located?"

"Oh, yes. I almost forgot. We're on the one hundred block of North Humphrey Avenue in Oak Park. One fifty-four North Humphrey, to be exact."

With that, Alex hung up without the slightest suggestion of a "good-bye."

The dye was now cast and the wheels set in motion. There was no turning back. There was no suitable alternative. Well, there was. However, that which lay on the "Fruit of the Looms" in his bedroom dresser drawer was more of a last resort than an alternative. As Alex wiped the beaded droplets of sweat and sodium chloride from his brow, he felt strangely nauseous and unsettled in the safe harbor of familiar and charted waters of his easy chair. Why had that simple telephone call had such a complex and conflicting effect on mind and body? What had been said, or not been said, that prodded the leviathan of the subconscious into sudden animation from the dormant state?

As the symphony directed by the synchrony between postural muscles and gravity soothed the physical, rumination and its older and wiser pal cerebration leapt into action. Alex tried to piece it all together. Oak Park. What the hell was Dr. Stawson doing in Oak Park? A physician of some stature would not maintain an office in Oak Park, at least not on the one hundred block of North Humphrey. Something was wrong. The Village of Oak Park, a once affluent suburb on the near Westside of Chicago, had already outlived its glory. Home to many of the creations of Frank Lloyd Wright, Oak Park was now a haven of the lower middleclass. Affirmative action, integration, resegregation, and the march of time itself had eroded the wealth of the Village. The winds of change had blown the rich further to the west and had taken the precious topsoil, that served as the heart and backbone of Oak Park, with them. All that remained was the chafe, and in the middle of all this the office and promise of salvation of Dr. Edward Stawson.

There was another possibility, however. Perhaps Dr. Stawson came from the countless ranks of foreign-trained physicians who had mercilessly invaded U.S. borders and shores for the last forty years. Those hordes of Indian, Pakistani, Chinese, Vietnamese, Korean, Mexican, Colombian, Cuban, African, Russian, and Arabic physicians who, while in many cases speaking barely a word of English when they had arrived in Shangri-La, nonetheless knew the value of a dollar and how to make one or two. With national origins, allegiances, and boundaries no longer clearly delineated in a complex, modern world, who could be sure of the nature of the beast. For all Alex knew, Dr. Stawson might have changed his name at some point, in order to corner an air of professional respectability inherent in a good ole Anglo-Saxon name. Office location would be a dead giveaway, though. If it were to become the sole judge and jury of the case, the verdict would most assuredly be guilty.

These and other misgivings filled Alex's psyche and a good part of his day. Three times he picked up the phone again and began dialing Dr. Stawson's number, obviously intent on canceling his appointment. Each time, something stronger than mind or matter stopped him in his tracks. The fact that the muscles of his hands and fingers refused to respond to conscious, cortical commands to place the cancellation call was the proof of God's existence, a sign of divine intervention to Alex. That meeting was destined to be, and neither all the bats in hell nor rain, sleet, or snow would deter him from the encounter with the good doctor. Only the Grim Reaper himself could rain on his party and cut short his date with immortality.

All that night Alex found it very difficult to sleep. His entire nervous system had been jolted by the events of the day, and no physiologic mechanism known or unknown to man could stem the flow of adrenaline's waters. Should he go to the appointment? What would he say to Dr. Stawson? Would he find Dr. Stawson to be a quack? Would the doctor promise him the moon? What would he do if the doctor could not deliver? Worst of all, how would his life change if the doctor could deliver? Questions and more questions, with no apparent answers. If Alex had, had a sleeping pill or tranquilizer for every thought that ran through his head that night, he could have sedated a good part of the City of Chicago. Hypnotics were not an option, however, as they would leave him drowsy. He had to be fresh in the morning. The only tried and true remedy at his disposal was the "island cure," a form of therapy that he had stumbled upon way back in college and perfected over the last four decades. It consisted of closing the eyes and imagining palm trees waving in the breeze on an uninhabited tropical island. Sleep induction usually followed rapidly.

Six a.m. It had worked. Now the quest for Avalon, the Holy Grail, Atlantis, and every other storybook adventure wonderland would have its beginning. Salvation was a mere bus and elevated train ride away. Alex skipped breakfast that morning. Food only dulled his senses; something about blood flow running to his stomach instead of his brain, where it would be much more needed and appreciated in a bind. He showered, shaved, and selected his best business suit for the morning's activities. Although his life might certainly be in shambles, his appearance at least would not be. Then, again, Dr. Stawson would probably be able to see through his charade, that is, if his medical degree and experience were genuine and not the product of some tabloid mail order house. No time to dwell on the matter. The time for action had come.

Alex was out the front door in a flash. A quick glance at his wristwatch told him that he would make his appointment with time to spare. He was pointed in the right direction, and there was a fair wind at his back. Now he could only hope that his decision to take bus and elevated train instead of car had been a sage one. Alex needed to think, and driving a car in Chicago's morning traffic was anything but thought provoking. It brought out the basest cogitations in the human reflection repertoire. So he caught a bus to the Downtown Loop, and there boarded the Lake Street elevated train for the trip west to Oak Park.

Alex had not ridden the Lake Street "el" for over twenty years. There had been something about it, passing through and above those slums and abandoned tenements, which had eventually repulsed him. It had been as if he were God, hovering above and observing the plight of mortal men. Powerful enough to act, and yet choosing not to do so. The slums would remain slums, and the men would remain mice. Meanwhile, everything would age and yet look much the same with the passage of time. Perhaps that was the very reason why Alex had taken the "el" that morning. It was his time machine. It was taking him to his date with destiny. He was going west to Oak Park to his Wizard of Oz, who would restore promise to his future by making him as ageless as the gutted buildings below.

The blurt of the loudspeaker and the conductor's voice interrupted Alex's train of thought, and would soon interrupt the train of his dreams. Austin Boulevard would be the next stop, and Alex prepared to get off the train and make the three-block walk to Dr. Stawson's office. The big and little hands of his timepiece indicated early arrival. Too early. No matter. He would get a cup of coffee at a local diner or something, and kill some time.

To his utter surprise, one block away from the train station at the busy intersection of Austin Boulevard and Lake Street, Alex realized that there were no diners, nor anything else for that matter. Greeting his arrival was a series of boarded-up buildings and failed businesses, for as far as the eye could see. Perhaps his decision to come all that way had not been a very wise one, after all. There was no turning back now, however. He had to see this thing through. Would the sight of desert sands have dissuaded King Arthur's knights from seeking the Holy Grail? Probably not, but the burned-out Kentucky Fried Chicken franchise and the three young, hungry black faces that approached him might have.

All he could do now was proceed. Intimidation would play no role in his private and personal adventure. Although sticks and stones might become a temporary inconvenience, Alex was simply too close now. In a worst case scenario, he would go down with the ship. In an eventual best of circumstances, he might wish he had. So, after an exchange of pleasantries and the payment of a ten dollar toll, Alex went on his way and let the youths go on theirs.

He rounded a corner and made for the middle of the next block, assuming that was where his treasure lay. Sure enough. One fifty-four North Humphrey. Was this all there was? Alex had certainly expected more than the three-story, multiunit apartment complex, which pained both eye and morale. Any physician worth his shingle would not have chosen this place to make a living. What had he done? Alex should have known better than to respond to that dubious ad in the newspaper. He had trusted his instincts, however. Those instincts, once keen and razor-sharp, had been dead for over thirty years now. What was he going to do? Images of a bedroom dresser drawer fluttered into and out of consciousness. A retracing of steps could only lead to a finger on trigger. He had to forge on. If his epitaph required proofreading, then let it be done there on North Humphrey Avenue. If destiny lay in the hands of a charlatan and burial ground in the midst of dilapidated mortar, then so be it.

Alex did the only thing a man in his position could do. He made his way to the street curb and sat down. There, he mustered every last ounce of business acumen, common sense, and gray matter to formulate a strategy. A decision had already been made. Rapid implementation was now the order of the day. His life would depend on it. As he stood up and braved the sudden, momentary dizziness brought on by blood collecting in his feet, Alex felt himself mysteriously drawn to the Wizard by some invisible force. A fleeting instant of lucidity was enough to convince him of the fact that he was nothing more than a passive pawn in a game of Ouija. Only movers and shakers are masters of their destinies, Alex thought. The rest of us slipstream.

As he entered the vestibule of the apartment complex, Alex could feel his right thigh begin to shake uncontrollably. The anticipation was just too much. He was a nervous wreck. His armpits were drenched, and he could barely breathe. He loosened his tie and licked his cracked lips. Onward.

Thirty-five, neatly typewritten names stood on the wall before him. To the left of each name was a small black doorbell. Alex skimmed the names rapidly. To his horror, he did not see "Dr. Stawson." Wait just one minute. His vision had been blurred. He would go through the list one more time. This time slowly. The Wizard just had to be there. Too much was riding on this spin of the wheel, and mechanical failure would mean total and unalterable capitulation. Concentrate, Alex. Scrutinize.

Perseverance and the benevolence of the gods paid off. For there, between the palm reader and the masseuse shone the name, "Dr. Edward Stawson." There was no "MD." or other sign of reassurance behind the name, but who cared. Dr. Stawson might even wear a string of shrunken heads around his neck, but after all he had been through, Alex would be glad to see him. As he raised his right arm to ring the doorbell, Alex surrendered to his fate. "My life is never going to be the same again," he mused.

"Yes," droned a female voice over the intercom system embedded in the vestibule wall. Alex immediately recognized the annoying tonality of the receptionist's voice. He was at the right place.

"Alex Bales to see Dr. Stawson, please."

"Come right up."

Alex was about to make his foray into what might turn out to be the netherworld, when he realized that he had not asked the floor number. He rang the doorbell again, this time underestimating his own strength and pushing the small button into the wall, where it became lodged. Chalk it up to old building syndrome, he thought.

"Yes," that same irritating voice.

"I'm sorry. I didn't get the floor."

"Third floor."

That terse reply was enough to open the starting gate, or perhaps the floodgates, and Alex was off like a flash. Nothing on this earth could have barred his way except the fact that the building did not possess an elevator. Three long flights of stairs would have to be negotiated, and Alex thanked his lucky stars he did not suffer from angina. At least, that. In another time, his mind would have most likely met Pompeii's end, while his heart sought nothing less than Rome's glory. As he reached the top of the first flight of stairs on his maiden voyage, he wondered what good fresh drinking water might have meant to a doomed passenger on the RMS Titanic.

Out of breath and with bright points of light flickering before his eyes, Alex finally arrived on the third floor. An involuntary curse left his lips. It served more as a catharsis than an exemplification of malcontent. His journey was nearly over. A couple of more feet and a couple of more minutes, and his questions would be answered. All his doubts would be erased.

Alex found himself in front of a solid oak door, eight feet high. Quite impressive. It was thick, bulletproof thick, from the look of it. Most assuredly, it had served past owners well in the days of speakeasies and bathtub gin. Now it was the only thing that stood between Alex and immortality. Crossing its threshold would be easy. There was no time to speculate on what lay afterward.

As he approached the door more closely, Alex saw the simple, unadorned "Edward Stawson" in two-inch, brass lettering. The "a" of "Stawson" appeared to have come loose, either from the march of time or conscious neglect. Whichever the case, it could not but portend an ill omen. Alex thought, "Oh, my God. What have I gotten myself into? 'A' for asshole. What kind of medical professional would leave such a blemished calling card. Dr. 'Stasshole,' of course."

He could wait no longer. It was now or never. Alex grabbed the brass doorknob, gave it a turn, and pushed. Nothing. The door did not budge. To make matters worse, there was neither doorbell nor knocker in sight. Alex momentarily flashed back to his bedroom dresser drawer. Suddenly and without warning, the biceps and triceps muscles of his right arm kicked into gear. He found himself beating furiously on this oak enemy. What could have been no more than seconds seemed like a prolonged engagement. With no quarter being given and surrender not an option, Alex was determined to break the door down or break a wrist in the process. He was seeing red, and saliva was foaming when the door popped open.

There, in all her glory, dressed in blue and draped in wrath, stood the king's champion. She would lay down her life without reservation before permitting this unholy infidel to desecrate the realm. Alex now understood why the ancient Pharaohs of Egypt had employed asps and cobras to guard the treasures of their burial chambers. Before a word could be uttered, mutual body language appeared to dictate a fight to the finish. As the combatants squared off for a verbal, if not physical, frontal assault, Alex regained both his composure and orientation to time and place.

"The good doctor is expecting me."

"I know."

"May I come in?"

Dr. Stawson's receptionist wore a navy blue business suit, which only served to accentuate the small balls of lint that had collected at the level of her pectoralis muscles. She was an imposing woman with hard facial features and a squint that would make even Clint Eastwood proud. Her appearance was definitely Eastern European, and Alex envisioned her as a gypsy queen earning the family's daily bread by directing pick-pocketing operations in Rome's Porta Portese market area. As she stepped aside to let him pass, Alex detected the pungent aroma of cheap perfume and perhaps a dash of whiskey. He could not help but think, as he crossed the threshold and noticed that her overuse of thick, red lipstick had transformed face into scowl, "I have entered Castle Dracula of my own free will."

Alex entered a 24-foot by 18-foot, rectangular waiting room. Nothing fancy, just extremely somber. The black and white photographs on the walls and the two dust-covered, oil paintings at the far end of the room, depicted Chicago in the early 1900s. Hardly the atmosphere for a doctor's office, but then, again, preferable to aseptic steel and muzak. Greens and browns were the prominent color schemes employed, and six high-backed, mahogany chairs stood against the right wall. Wrist and ankle restraints and crowns of metal and wires were all that was needed to make them resemble electric chairs.

The left wall was punctuated by a large oak desk and a doorway. Would Alex find Dr. Jekyll or Mr. Hyde beyond that door? No matter. Either one might become his savior. Their methods would certainly be different, but the end-result most likely the same. He had come this far. It was now time to see this thing through, come what may.

"Please have a seat. The doctor will see you very shortly..."

Alex could not be sure if he had heard her add, "...that is, if you can behave yourself." The last few minutes had done nothing to relieve the tension between them, created by the previous door-pounding episode.

The receptionist took her place at the desk, and tried to regain some degree of composure and professional demeanor by thumbing through some loose papers. Her irritation, however, was obvious, and her bearing was more suited to a matron in a high-security, women's prison facility. Alex could read the name, "Marie Comanescu, R.N.," written plainly on the nameplate that lay on her desk. He entertained a perverse thought. "So, she is a nurse. I guess Dr. Josef Mengele had nurses, too."

Seated there in Dr. Stawson's waiting room, Alex's gaze darted from one object to another. The rhythmic movements of his eyes denuded everything in their path, except, of course, Nurse Comanescu. Her undressing, both literal and figurative, would be left to either an unlucky husband or a superhero fit to look upon the face of Medusa.

Having dissected his surroundings down to the bone, Alex now turned his attention and his analytic mind to the marrow of the place. Several times he found the browns and greens of the room transporting him back to the cheap pool halls he had frequented as a teenager.

The distant sound of a pull on a door brought him back to reality. From the look on Nurse Comanescu's face, Alex realized that it was now time for him to cross yet another threshold.

Milliseconds seemed like seconds, and seconds, in turn, seemed like minutes. As he closed the door behind himself and stood before a being who resembled a cross between Sigmund Freud and a leprechaun, Alex felt the jumpstart of his inner demons and poisons. "Make me an offer," he thought he heard himself say.

4

Too Good to be True

The emaciated Dr. Stawson looked up from the mound of paperwork, which lay before him on his all but tidy desk. That piece of archaic furniture, to be sure, had seen better days. So, too, had Edward Stawson. A frail attempt at a smile, which was much more akin to a smirk, and the telltale glint of two blinking eyes were the closest thing to a red carpet welcome that Alex had received in a long time. Although his first impression of the good doctor's appearance and demeanor was nothing to write home about, these were desperate times and Alex would reserve judgment. After all, he, too, was no sight for sore eyes. For a moment, closer scrutiny of Dr. Stawson's face, as he rose to greet his new guinea pig, revealed what might have been a mirror image of himself in the play of the light.

"Mr. Bales, I presume."

"Dr. Stawson, I presume."

There was no exchange of small-talk, nor would there be in the future. No niceties. No cup of coffee. No smiling secretary to bring in a tray of pastries. Both men were there for business, and both knew it. Alex could not help but think that he had seen Dr. Stawson somewhere before. Stawson's seventy years, his wry and wiry frame, cue ball scalp, and that touch of the equivocal made him a fitting character for a Hitchcock movie or a suitable foil to dupe even the keenest Humphrey Bogart, Dashell Hammet, or Sam Spade.

"Please, be seated, Mr. Bales. I'll be with you in a moment. I won't waste any of your precious time. We'll get down to business shortly."

There was something odd about Dr. Stawson's delivery. Although his English was perfect and his grammar and syntax correct, a slight Eastern European accent was nonetheless unmistakable. Alex could not quite place his presumed savior's national origin, but the Czech Republic, Hungary, Poland, Rumania, and Transylvania were all good guesses. Perhaps Stawson and his receptionist were a brother and sister pair, or even "kissing cousins." Alex took devilish delight in the last thought, so much so that a crude hint at a smile forced his dried lips apart ever so slightly.

For Alex, one fact was beyond confutation, whether there be proof or not. It was in the cards and in the stars that Edward Stawson was a Jew. Not that Alex had anything against Jews. His best friend as a youth had been Jewish, and he had long ago come to respect their drive and intelligence. He knew they made fine physicians, although sometimes a bit on the greedy side. Perhaps "Stawson" had been "Stawsky," "Stawsonsky," or "Stawsonovich" in some past life. No matter. This was now, and that would be the one stone that Alex would leave unturned. Perhaps as a child, Dr. Stawson had seen horrors that, by comparison, would make a Chicago inner-city riot or gang fight look like a tea party. Hopefully, scarring would not be a major part of Edward Stawson's psychological repertoire, nor would he continue Dr. Mengele's unfinished work on Alex, as the former's heir apparent.

Two minutes passed, and Alex grew impatient to begin. Two minutes can seem an eternity when a life hangs in the balance. And let there be no mistake. A life did. Finally, Dr. Stawson dropped his pen to the desk, looked up, and began what would be, for Alex, the most important oral dissertation of his mortal existence. All would not go smoothly, however, as Alex was soon to learn.

"Clinical research," exhorted Edward Stawson, "must perforce pass through three obligatory stages..."

"Spare me the preamble to your Nobel acceptance speech," blurted Alex suddenly, "and get to the point."

If looks could kill, Alex would have been vaporized on the spot by the glare in Stawson's eyes. If there was one thing the good doctor did not tolerate, it was interruption by an impertinent patient. Dr. Stawson had long ago been schooled in proper etiquette by Old World masters, who would have considered Emily Post wet behind the ears. Furthermore, Stawson, like Alex, had a short fuse. So, if one were to believe that opposites attract, then it would have appeared that Stawson and Alex had made the journey from the furthest, diametrically opposed reaches of the universe to inhabit the same point in time for a reason. Fuses would eventually fizzle out. Bipolar disorder would not, and both were afflicted to a greater or lesser extent.

"Now, before I was so rudely interrupted," Dr. Stawson began again, "I..."

"I sure hope you're going to cut the crap and get on board quickly."

"Mr. Bales, what the hell is your problem?"

"I'm dying, Doctor. That is my problem, and your chitchat is interfering with an appointment I must keep with a dresser drawer."

"A dresser drawer?"

"A pistol in a dresser drawer."

At that point, Edward Stawson realized that the situation was indeed grave. Desperate times, however, would not dictate a shortcut to correct methodology. He would continue to pursue his course of action in a logical manner, and in doing so would win the day for himself, science, and the unfortunate creature in the chair opposite him. Should things go badly, it did not matter. Stawson's greatness would never be recognized in his lifetime anyway, and human guinea pigs were a dime a dozen. With thirty-three percent of the U.S. population clinically depressed, his practice would never be wanting for takers or gamblers willing to risk all for the promise of immortality. Whether his elixir of youth could deliver, or not, was not the point. Although he honestly believed it could, the potion itself was merely a secondary consideration. Of much greater significance was the fact that in his drab, little office in a suburb of Chicago that had seen better times, Edward Stawson held the power of life and death in his hands. A wrong word, unconscious gesture, or unnoticed mannerism on his part could put a final nail in a coffin or make front-page news.

Legal responsibility on his shoulders? No, there was none. Moral dilemmas? Marginal. Most of humanity's feces left on his doorstep had long ago ceased to enrich earth's green pastures. Most of his human guinea pigs already had one foot in the grave. Terminality, Dr. Stawson often thought, gives one license to ignore socially and morally acceptable norms of practice. With that in mind and armed with a philosophy that Hippocrates would hardly have approved of, Stawson set to work on the unpleasant task before him.

"Mr. Bales, if you'll just be patient for a moment and let me explain my research, methodology, and clinical procedures, I'm more than certain that you will leave my office a happier man than when you walked through the door."

"Okay. Okay. But make it fast."

"As I had already begun to explain to you, clinical research studies generally involve three obligatory stages, termed phase I, phase II, and phase III. Now, I am not going to bore you with the details of phase I and phase II studies. I know that you are not here for that. Whether you knew it or not, however, phase III was what drew you to my office via my newspaper ad."

"All right. I'll bite. So? What is phase III?"

"Mr. Bales, a phase III research study is a large-scale evaluation of a drug's safety and potency. It is usually conducted at numerous sites around the country or around the world, for that matter. Many human subjects, numbering in the hundreds or sometimes even in the thousands, are generally involved."

"Thank you for the Biology 101 lesson, Dr. Stawson, but can we move on?"

"In my study, only fifty subjects will be involved. Two groups of twenty-five each. None of the subjects will ever meet or come into contact in any way with the others. If you decide to join my phase III clinical trial, Mr. Bales, you will be randomly assigned to one of the two groups of twenty-five. Furthermore, the trial will be randomized, placebo-controlled, and double-blind."

"Cut the mumbo-jumbo, Doc, and give it to me plain."

"The randomized part I think you understand. Two groups of twenty-five, and you'll be assigned to one of the two. One group will receive my new drug, FOY1, while the other will get a placebo or dummy pill. It's just that simple, and I want you to be clear on that point. The chance of your getting FOY1 is only fifty percent, Mr. Bales."

"Hold it, right there."

"No, Mr. Bales, you hold it, right there. Let me finish."

"But..."

"No 'buts.' I'm giving it to you plain and simple, and I expect you to let me finish before registering any of your complaints or objections. Now, as I was saying, the chance of your getting my new treatment is only fifty percent. And here is something else I'm sure you're not going to like. To ensure unequivocal test results and safeguard against investigator or subject bias, neither you nor I, Mr. Bales, will know which group you are in. That's what we mean when we say that the clinical trial is double-blind."

The look of utter loss and desperation, forged indelibly into Alex's already well-worn facial features, gave Dr. Stawson reason to pause. This was no longer a two-way conversation, but rather an imposed soliloquy on his part. And just as Alex's right biceps cocked reflexively in anticipation of a throwing in of the towel, Stawson began again.

"Now for the good news, Mr. Bales. I am going to pick up the entire tab for the clinical trial. You don't have to pay a thing."

That was simply too much for old Alex to bear. He could contain himself no longer. Stawson's last utterances had reeked of used-car salesman, circus sideshow barker, or elixir vendor. With a move that would have made a cobra proud, Alex lurched from his sedentary position to one of attack. He did not feel his two massive, sweaty palms envelope the muscles and internal carotid arteries of the good doctor's neck. Were it not for the sound of glass shattering in an ashtray's flight from Dr. Stawson's desk, Alex might have completed the dirty deed. As it were, a return to reality brought the sight of the doctor gasping for breath, as well as a shrill scream and look of horror and utter despair on the face of Stawson's receptionist.

Alex tried to move his lips in an attempt to explain. No use. Nothing would come out. Dr. Stawson reached for a glass of water. He had to create some kind of airway in a throat that had all but collapsed. As Alex, again, tried to speak, the doctor beat him to the punch. Stawson raised his left hand, as if to say "Stop." and hastened the flow of water into his mouth with his right. A sudden move of his hand from the vertical to the horizontal, and a change in direction to indicate the door, sealed Alex's fate. The dye had been cast. There was nothing more to do than slowly fade into the sunset. A sunset that promised a long overdue appointment with a dresser drawer.

As Alex turned and made his way to the door, he was suddenly overcome by the urge to look back. He would not do so, however. Something far more deadly than Medusa's face, or the pillar of stone he might transform into, would greet retroaction. No, Alex's only viable courses of action were surrender and humiliation. The first, already a logical certainty. The second, adding insult to injury. It was now full speed ahead to a rendezvous point where a millisecond's flash of powder would erase the acute pain of the last six months, and arrest the toxic, existential metastases of the last forty years. At least power over the time and place of the Grim Reaper's embrace had remained in his corner.

Three more steps and he would be out the door. No more decisions to make. Just a long taxi ride with price no object. In a couple of hours, a short journey in the direction opposite the tunnel of white light would signal an end to earthly pain. Hurt of another kind would supplant it, but, Alex thought, it could not be any worse and might even be pleasurable.

As he lifted his right leg, his right hand going instinctively for the door-knob, Alex became suddenly paralyzed by a force transcending the laws of physics. Ah, the power of the mind. Or was it the soul that had suddenly kicked in? No matter. Alex stopped dead in his tracks and was overcome by a crippling wave of futility and inertia. He could feel its crest come crashing down, and his fear and defenselessness became manifest in his guttural and convulsed sobbing. He must have sounded more like a wounded animal, or something not of this earth, than a mere mortal in the throes of desperation.

After what seemed like an interminable length of time, but may have amounted to only a minute and a half, Alex was prepared to continue on his journey. Embarrassment and acknowledgment had never been factors, as he had not looked back to see the horrified expressions on the faces of the good doctor and his faithful receptionist. As impetus was applied to his fragile chassis, Alex felt a gentle hand on his left shoulder impede his getaway. He turned to see Dr. Stawson, with a fatherly, sympathetic look in his eyes, motion him back to the safety of the womb and his office.

"Mr. Bales, I will give you FOY1. The hell with my study. The hell with all studies!"

Alex did not know what to say at this point. So, he simply acquiesced, and let the doctor go on. With a gesture of his right arm, Dr. Stawson indicated the door to his inner sanctum, and signaled his receptionist that her services would no longer be needed. Whether the doctor felt he could handle the situation alone, or simply preferred no witnesses for what he was about to say, made little difference. Alex welcomed the woman's departure. She had already seen much, too much.

"Have a seat, Mr. Bales. You and I have many matters to discuss, and the afternoon is short. You will never be the same after you hear what I am about to say. So, Mr. Bales, you must decide once and for all. Are you in or out?"

"Whether your true name be Dr. Stawson, Dr. Faustus, Dr. Jekyll, Dr.

Frankenstein, Beelzebub, Mephistopheles, or Attila the Hun, I am in. I have absolutely nothing more to lose. I've lost my best and only friend. I have no life."

"Mr. Bales, how do you feel about getting old?"

"Age, Doctor? What are a few wrinkles, more or less."

"Age, Mr. Bales, can be a state of mind as well as body. I can help you with the latter. Only you can exorcise the demons in your mind. Let there be no mistake, Mr. Bales, the mission you are about to embark on, with me as your guide, is no less sacred than the quest for the Holy Grail or the eternal struggle between Good and Evil. You will be my guinea pig, and I will be your god. You will execute my every whim, even the strangest. In doing so, Mr. Bales, rest assured that you will be reversing the cancers of both the mind and body. I will take you back in time, and you will take me and mankind forward. Is that clear?"

Alex nodded. The good doctor's mysticism and cryptic presentation, however, were utterly lost on a mind that had gone through so many deleterious changes in the last forty years, six months, and fifteen minutes.

Dr. Stawson carefully scrutinized the monotonic body language of his two-legged guinea pig. There were no further signs of emotion on the part of Alex, and this preoccupied Stawson. No tremors, goose bumps, tics, or telltale twitches. Just acquiescence and passive acceptance. Stawson, ever the artist, would impart form to this mass of clay, but Alex, and Alex alone, would be responsible for breathing life into the doctor's creation.

"Do you have any questions, Mr. Bales?"

"No, Dr. Frankenstein."

It was good to see, all things considered, that Alex had not lost his sarcastic sense of humor. Perhaps this entire affair would not become a total fiasco after all, thought Dr. Stawson. He had learned long ago that nothing could compromise successful and auspicious completion of even the most well designed research study than substandard materie prime.

"Good. Then let's begin. There are things I need to tell you, and things you need to hear. If it is all right with you, I will call you 'Alex,' and you may call me 'Edward.'"

A moment of silence followed. In that instant, both men realized that the stage had been set, the actors were in place, and, for better or worse, the curtain would be going up shortly.

"Now, Alex, in the next three decades, the number of individuals in this country over 85 years of age is going to almost double from twenty-nine million to over fifty-one million. I'm most certainly not going to be around to see this, but you may be. Are you absolutely certain that you wish to take part in my experiment? Once we begin, there will be no turning back. To do so would result in hazardous consequences to both your mind and body."

"Doc, if you're trying to scare me, you're wasting your time. I have nothing to lose. I already have one foot in the grave. Losing my balance is something I take for granted."

"All right, Alex. We'll do this thing. It's not going to be easy, though. It would perhaps be easier to clone a human being with reptilian skin qualities than change the proverbial leopard's spots, or turn back the hands of time. Water to wine is child's play, in comparison."

"Save your proselytizing for souls that can be saved. Mine was lost long before I walked through your door. Let's get on with it."

Although Edward Stawson knew that Alex was in no way suited to begin the experiment at that moment, his hands were tied. On the other hand, Alex might be just the subject he needed, someone with nothing to lose. Yet, there was something about this man, some inner nobility, which beckoned Stawson to put on the brakes. Surely, science would not be served by the sacrifice of an already broken man. What if it worked, however. It probably would not, but what if it did. At that point, what better standard bearer than Alex Bales.

Edward stared intensely into Alex's clouded eyes, and slowly began, "Here is what I propose to do. Now, Alex, please don't interrupt me. You can ask all the questions you want when I have finished."

Alex's silence was an invitation to proceed.

"I stumbled across FOY1 purely by accident. You needn't be concerned how. Your only concern should be what you will do if my creation works. There is a chance, albeit a slim one, that it will. That scenario might not signal an end to your nightmare, but just the beginning. Alex, if you've been unable to live your life satisfactorily as an older man, what makes you think you can do so as a young man again?"

Still more silence.

"Don't answer that. Let me go on. FOY1, which stands for 'Fountain of Youth 1,' should ease your depression, Alex. It's no secret that people over age 65 have a high incidence of depression and commit suicide at a rate higher than any other age group in the U.S. Before you become a statistic, I wish to place you on a biweekly regimen of my so-called elixir. It can't hurt you, Alex. At least, I don't think it can. Will it help? Probably not, but then again, it might. Nothing is ever a given in love, war, or medicine."

Stawson was on a roll, and Alex's newfound reticence was music to his ears.

"FOY1 should increase stomach activity and blood flow, bowel motility, and digestion. The bottom-line is that it will most likely improve your gastrointestinal tract. Furthermore, I think it will increase your body water, muscle mass, and protein levels. All pluses. What age has taken away from you, my little magic bullet should restore."

"Enough bullshit, Doc. Now tell me what I want to hear."

"Okay, okay. Here it is. Will FOY1 make you look and feel younger, Alex? God only knows. I have never fully tested it on all aspects of the aging process. You are going to be like that first chimpanzee sent by the Russians into outer space. If something goes terribly wrong, like the monkey there will be no bringing you back safely. But I wouldn't dwell on that. I am more than certain that some of the drug's effects will be those you desire."

Alex was about to interrupt again, but Stawson was now like a runaway locomotive. He would risk derailment in the process of getting his point across.

"The liver is an extremely important organ, and FOY1's effects on it are irrefutable. On my experimental regimen, I fully expect your liver blood flow to increase by about 40%, your liver size to increase in relation to the rest of your body, and your liver's metabolism and energy production to increase at least twofold. Not only that, but simultaneous improvement in your kidney function should be a welcome bonus. Alex, your kidneys will increase their waste disposal rate, and there will be a cleansing of all that, if you'll excuse the word, "crap" and toxic poison accumulated over the years in your body. In short, if we are what we eat, you should look and feel much younger on the outside for what we have disposed of from the inside. Now, Alex, do you have any questions?"

Alex looked completely bewildered. He had slumped in his chair during the doctor's oratory. Beads of sweat coalesced into rivulets on his forehead. His throat was parched, and his tongue dry. However, a spark of curiosity had been engaged.

"Doc, I haven't understood a God damn thing you've said. Just tell me one thing. Will this miracle cure of yours work, or not?"

"I honestly don't know, Alex. I can tell you that if I were a betting man, and I'm not, I certainly wouldn't bet on it. On the other hand, do you have any other real choice?"

Alex closed his eyes. He knew that his answer would be forthcoming shortly. Until then, he chose to roam that tropical island in his mind, where blues and greens were as hemlock to inner demons and blended nicely into tones, shades, and hues of significant therapeutic value. Virgin beaches, crystal-clear waters, magnificent palm trees, and a burgeoning flora and fauna exerted momentary beneficent effects on a spirit long ago polluted by the toil of daily existence. Several seconds of such therapy could eradicate decades of mental torment, but only temporarily. The clearing of a throat, the drop of a pin, or the sound of a car horn in the street below could induce relapse at a moment's notice.

"Well, Alex, have you made up your mind?"

Those words served as a reality check, and transported Alex back to the world of the living. No more tropical island paradise. No more basking in the bliss of peaceful unreality. Two beady eyes, a long, hooked nose, and a frown were all trained on Alex now, and they demanded an answer.

"When do we begin, Doc?"

"One week from today. Eight o'clock sharp."

5

The Proposal

One week later, at eight a.m. sharp, Alex once again found himself before his master and savior. Not Jesus Christ, but Edward Stawson. Alex would follow any path dictated by the latter. He knew that. His only hope was that the journey would be short and sweet. Pain would not be a factor. It could not. He had already suffered so much that pinpricks, injections, and other corporeal invasions could be nothing more than strictly academic. Alex was about to embark on his voluntary adventure with a one-way ticket, purchased not with hard currency, but with life's blood. His inner serenity was not at stake. That had been lost long ago. His life was not in danger. That he should fear the loss of something, which had absolutely no value for him, was ludicrous at best.

So, Alex would forge on. He was determined to do so. A card shark he was not, but he would play his best hand. And, if the hand dealt him by Edward Stawson were to be a losing one, there would be no further chips to cash in and no need to check out. The game was to be played for keeps. Winning, for Alex, might mean losing all.

There he sat, for what appeared to be an eternity to his dulled senses. In reality, it amounted to about five minutes, more or less. The man who would push the buttons was seated before him. Stolid, perceptive, discerning, ambiguous, disconcerting, and, above all, dubious all came to mind. Could Edward Stawson do it? Doubtful, thought Alex. Did it matter? Not in the least. A result would be had, and the experiment would be a success, even if that, simply stated, meant the advancement of scientific knowledge at the expense of a simpleton's mortal soul.

It was now or never. Alex was ready. As he stared intensely across that old, wooden desk at what could have been mistaken for a magical being in times of yore, Alex became impressed by the play of colors. Edward Stawson, adorned by the symbols of his office, was trussed up in tight-fitting, brown surgical garb that gave him the appearance of either high priest or Egyptian mummy. How apropos, Alex mused. Here he had come expecting to see the greens of asepsis, cleanliness, and life, only to be greeted with the browns of autumn. Was he missing something here? Was this a foreshadowing of some kind? Would autumn precede his winter, his death?

That last week had gone by so quickly. It had begun slowly, almost lethargically, and had built to a feverish crescendo culminating here in this particular point in time and space. Although Alex had grown restive on more than one occasion in the last one hundred and sixty-eight hours, he had managed to keep his emotions in check. In fact, he had been happier than he could ever remember. A semblance of hope had been extended to him, and he had resolved to cling to it for dear life. It would most certainly keep him afloat in his current ocean of woe, and it might even be taken for granted or relegated to the realm of the subconscious henceforth, with Captain Stawson at the helm.

Movement in the good doctor's lips brought Alex back to the here and now.

"How are you feeling today, my lad?"

"As well as can be expected, under the circumstances. Are we going to dispense with the niceties and get down to business?"

"Patience is a noble virtue, my boy. Kingdoms have been built on it, and empires have been crushed in its absence. Did Alexander the Great rush into his conquest of the world?"

"But he was only thirty-three, Stawson, when the world lay at his feet. I'm a little older than that, and my time is running out. I no longer have an upper hand on my own inner demons, let alone the minds and souls of other wayfarers on this planet."

"You, too, Alex, will once again have your thirty-three years, but it will be important how you use them. I'm going to give you a second chance, and I don't want you to blow it. That is why I wish to take the time now to explain the ground rules."

"Is this absolutely necessary, Doc?"

"You bet it is. Let's put it this way. If you don't tow the line right now and hear me out, then you might as well walk out that door immediately and never come back."

Edward Stawson's voice and demeanor had taken on a tone of agitation. He was much more somber than Alex had ever seen him. It became quite clear that the old codger meant business, and that he was not going to play mind games with his guinea pig. Alex would listen, absorb, and remember. Nothing more, nothing less. His mentor would pronounce, and he would commit to memory. Anything short of this would not be tolerated, as evidenced by the squint in Stawson's eyes and the frown on his face. Alex realized, in the course of but a few minutes, that this was to be a mental and physical dictatorship, with the mad doctor at the controls. The course laid would inevitably be Alex's, but the all-important provisioning would be left up to Stawson.

"Okay, Doc, you win. Let's get on with it."

"Alex, we are not going to begin until I set the record straight here, and tell you exactly what we are going to do. I must explain the salient points of the procedure to you. I must make sure that you understand their full ramifications. To do anything less would not be a personal violation, but might even be construed as a crime against humanity."

"You have my attention. Go on."

Stawson recognized a glint of purpose in Alex's eyes, and realized that it was now or never. Carpe diem. He must be brief, clear, and to the point. A man's life would depend on diction and enunciation. Words must not be wasted. Body language and gestures must be perfect. The idea that failure would not be an option must be impressed upon Alex. If there was any doubt as to the successful completion of the experiment, it would have to be addressed immediately. To do so later would mandate abortion of the procedure, or worse.

"Alex, you must listen to me carefully. What I am about to say will become Holy Scripture for you. The Word. You will live by it, and learn from it. In fact, your entire future existence will be a reflection of what you are about to hear and learn in the next five minutes. Are we clear on this point?"

"Crystal. Go on. Go on."

Dr. Stawson became aware that he had gained Alex's full attention. So, he wasted no further time and proceeded to the heart of the matter.

"Every Monday of every week for the next three months, you will be given a small twenty milliliter, intravenous injection of FOY1. The injection will be painful, Alex. Your body will react to the drug, but I can assure you that I will do everything in my power to lessen all unpleasant side effects. That is all I can guarantee. Anything more would be a lie."

Alex did not bat an eyelash, but leaned forward in his chair as if he was about to respond. He thought better, however, and returned to a more comfortable posture. Stawson took that as a cue to continue his discourse.

"Three months, no more, no less, will be necessary to stop and completely reverse the aging process. You will begin to feel the beneficial effects of FOY1 at about the halfway point. If all goes as planned, you should begin to feel and look somewhat younger at that point. Your vision will improve dramatically, and energy levels will increase by leaps and bounds thereafter. Sexual prowess will parallel that of a very young adult, and there will not be an organ system or tissue left untouched by FOY1. Am I being perfectly clear? Are you still with me, Alex?"

"Say what you have to say, Doc. Let's get this over with."

"Don't dismiss me so cavalierly, Alex."

"I'm not, Doc. I just want to get started."

"I can assure you, Alex, that your undivided attention, patience, and cooperation now will prevent future doubts and unpleasant mishaps. As I was saying, no organ or tissue will escape the beneficial effects of FOY1. You will feel better and look much younger. Your strength and muscle tone will increase, and your memory will improve one hundredfold. Women will adore you for your cleverness and quick wit, and you will be able to once again satisfy their every sexual whim and desire without the aid of little blue pills, pumps, or other paraphernalia. In short, Alex, you will be my creation, my new Frankenstein monster, so to speak. I will give you a new, second life and a new beginning. In return, I ask for nothing, at least for now."

Alex listened as best he could, small beads of perspiration encircling the circumference of his head like the ring of a crown on a man who would once again be king.

Then he interjected, "But wait just one minute, Dr. Stawson. This all sounds a little too good to be true. Now, I am fully aware that I am not playing with a full deck of cards at this moment, nor have I been for quite some time. Nonetheless, Doc, do you honestly expect me to believe that benevolence in my regard is your sole motivation for acting. Do you take me for a fool? Sick, maybe, but a fool, never."

"Alex, believe whatever you wish. If you feel that ulterior motives are a factor here, then, by all means, stick to your guns. Don't give up on yourself or my experiment, though. I know this is going to sound trite, but you truly have everything to gain by trusting me."

"In Italy, they say that trust is a good thing, but not trusting is better. 'Fidarsi è buono ma non fidarsi è meglio.'"

"Where I come from, Alex, we say that trust is a beautiful thing. So, what's it going to be? There is no more time to waste. Are you with me, or not?"

Edward Stawson ceased all verbal communication at that point. He would say no more until a final decision was made. The ball was now in Alex's court, and Alex knew it. Would he save the day and become a hero, or would he miss the final shot and go down in defeat and humiliation? A split second from now his decision would come, and only God would know how he reached it. Alex certainly would not.

He took a deep breath, and his fate was sealed. Alex would follow Stawson into hell, if need be.

"Okay Doc, you win."

Both Alex and the good doctor knew that in a matter of minutes a one-way path was to be followed, from which there would be no return. Nothing would ever be the same for either one of them. Alex, if all went well, would embark upon a new adventure, a new life. Edward Stawson, on the other hand, would quietly observe the fate of his constructed prodigy or hapless victim, whichever the case might be. He would draw vicarious pleasure or horror from a life that he himself could not live. His human guinea pig would actually be at the helm, and the maestro, the creator of this physiologic concerto, would only be along for the ride.

"Shall we, Alex?"

"Let's do it, Doc."

"Do you have any questions? Do you want further explanations?"

"No, Doc, I guess the countdown began some time ago. Let's just see if we can get this thing off the ground."

"All right, then."

Without further fanfare, Dr. Stawson beckoned Alex to follow him through a pair of double doors on the far end of his office. They entered a dimly lit, adjacent anteroom, which served as both storage space and a medical library of sorts. To Alex, this entire affair was, indeed, taking on the flavor of a Frankenstein story more and more. But who cared. He had given his word. He had taken what amounted to a blood oath. If the mind was willing, then so, too, must be the body. Having followed the doctor into this zone of crepuscular deliverance, Alex now found that he could no longer lift his feet. An element of fear had begun to chip away at his resolve, and course navigation would now have to proceed by shuffling gait, in much the same way as waters charted by Parkinsonian patients.

Edward Stawson immediately recognized the hesitation in his protégé's manner and the dropped cadence in his step.

"Don't be afraid, my boy, we're almost there."

And with the flick of a switch and the flash of a spark, an entire wall of tomes parted, and Alex found himself in the "Land of Oz."

This experiment would not be conducted behind the aseptic walls of a conventional hospital or clinic, but rather in the bowels of a dilapidated, old building in an abandoned neighborhood on the west side of Chicago, by a high priest of some sort.

"Please, Alex, come into my examination room."

As he heeded the call, Alex became momentarily blinded by the strong, fluorescent lights and hypnotized by the continuous drone of telemetry, monitors, servers, and a corner mainframe. What had he gotten himself into? There was much more to Edward Stawson than had originally met the eye. Could this place be Purgatory, where Alex and the sins of his past life would be placed on exhibit for all to see? Or was it rather more akin to an operating theater, where his very soul would be exchanged for a virgin, though not kindred, spirit to be later unleashed on an unsuspecting world?

"Don't mind all the toys. They're not for you, at least not for now. You're here for a simple injection, Alex."

"Buzzers and bells are fine, Doc, if that's what you need to have. I just wasn't expecting such an elaborate web."

"Web?"

"C'mon, Doc. Don't play stupid with me. I'm not going to run away. I am your proverbial fly, and you are going to do with me what you will."

Stawson thought better than to open that can of worms. A response, albeit a sympathetic one, would just feed the fires. The proper tack in this case would be silence. A silence of several minutes, to rejuvenate the psyche, reestablish neural networks, and calm the raging waters, would be just what the doctor ordered. Then, again, the better part of prudence might be action, and perhaps the dénouement should be accelerated at this point. What to do? What to do?

Alex was not the only subject in Stawson's experiment, nor would he be the last. And yet, the doctor felt a kinship, a particular camaraderie of sorts, with him that transcended standard operating procedure and the established norms for physician-patient relationships. Dr. Stawson could help this man, and he knew it. Turning his back on his patient at this point would be tantamount to making a reservation for Alex at the Cook County Morgue.

So, the silence between them persisted for what appeared to be hours. In reality, it was only minutes. It was Alex now who would have to take the initiative. The doctor felt that he himself could not. Alex would have to make the crucial move in this mortal game of chess. Could he do it? Would he do it? Stawson had his doubts. Yet his patient and shadow of a man had demonstrated considerable resilience in the face of adversity, especially in the last six months.

As each tick of the clock added a day to Edward Stawson's age, he was nonetheless certain that Alex would soon demonstrate some sign of life. Whether it would be in the form of a remonstrance, a capitulation, an acceptance, or a confession made little difference to the doctor at this point. The tension was killing him. He needed an answer, and he needed it now. Patience had been one of Stawson's strong points in his youth, but the march of time had cast it to the wind. His ruminations and mental calisthenics were suddenly interrupted by what seemed to be distant murmurings, which brought him back to the reality of the moment.

"...nevertheless, Doc, it's probably a little too late to turn back now. I guess I'm still game, if you are."

Without giving much thought to what he would say next, Dr. Stawson found himself motioning Alex to the examination table.

"Take off your shirt, my lad, and let's give you the once over before your journey begins."

Stawson did a cursory, but thorough, physical of his resigned patient. Vital signs were all in order, and muscle tone and superficial and deep reflexes appeared to be normal. In fact, they were much better than expected for a man

Alex's age, and that was quite encouraging. Perhaps, thought Dr. Stawson, Alex's physical condition might compensate somewhat for obvious deficits in the psychological realm. Next, Stawson drew some blood as a precautionary measure. Though the experiment would begin that very day, the results of those blood tests, a week from then, would determine the continuation or the termination of Alex's voyage back to the future. They might even detail or curtail the eventual duration of his remaining time here on earth.

After approximately an hour and a half of poking, prodding, pricking, and questioning, the good doctor was more than satisfied with the preliminaries. The experiment could now proceed as planned, that is, if Alex did not get cold feet and bail out. All systems were "go" at this point, and Stawson felt that he must let his "astronaut" know it.

"Alex, are you ready?"

Alex's throat felt suddenly dry, as he realized this was it. Dr. Stawson did not have to go into the specifics of the physical exam. The look on Alex's face acknowledged comprehension of the fact that he had checked out okay There was no need for verbal expression of the matter.

"All right, Doc, do your thing. Hurry up, before I change my mind."

Stawson moved quickly, yet methodically, toward a large, stainless steel refrigerator in a corner of the examination room. Alex thought to himself, "That must be Fort Knox, where the Ol' Doc stockpiles his magic potion."

He kept a keen, fixed eye on the doctor's movements. He did not wish to miss a thing. What did this elixir look like? How long had it taken to prepare and develop it? Could it produce any adverse side effects? Had it ever been tested on animals or other human beings? These and many other more sinister questions flooded the limited functional space of Alex's cranial cavity. He knew, however, that he would not voice his concerns. The already evident waste of precious time precluded that. Besides, although Alex did not know Stawson well, there had always been something in the doctor's manner and demeanor that commanded both trust and respect.

As Edward Stawson turned to face Alex from the far end of the room, a small vial containing a fluorescent green fluid became immediately evident in the doctor's right hand. The symbolism was not wasted on Alex. Right hand meant life. Had the liquid been toted in the doctor's left, second thoughts might have arisen.

"This is your last chance, Alex. Once we begin, there will be no turning back."

As Alex presented his right arm for injection, he thought to himself, "What does Stawson mean, 'no turning back?' Surely, he can't be serious. I can terminate the experiment any time I want. It's my decision, my life, and my choice."

"Fire away, Doc."

Stawson pushed Alex's right arm away, and took firm hold of his left with his own left hand. A split second later, Alex felt the tightening of a latex tourniquet around his upper left arm. "Left arm, huh," he thought, perhaps something sinister is about to happen, after all." He could not help but notice the doctor's extremely serious and somber facial expression, as he inserted the small-bore syringe needle through the wall, and into the lumen, of a dilated vein near the junction of Alex's left arm and forearm. A painstakingly slow process of injection of twenty milliliters of the eerily toned, fluorescent green, FOY1 fluid followed. Speed was not, and could not be, at a premium here, as Dr. Stawson knew full well that any carelessness or rapidity of infusion might result in a gross hematoma or extravasation of the elixir into the surrounding tissues. Subsequent compromise of the anticipated or successful clinical outcome might then follow. It therefore became imperative that both doctor and patient be on their toes, as vigilance was the name of the game.

After what seemed to Alex to be an interminable length of time, but amounted to only three minutes, to be exact, the needle was withdrawn. The journey had now begun in earnest. He was no longer a passive bystander, but an active participant. The good doctor looked at him inquisitively, wishing to ask Alex any number of questions, but thought better not to do so at that moment. For the next three months, Alex would have to concentrate all his energy and all his faculties selfishly on himself. The transition must be smooth. The transformation from frog to tadpole must occur without a glitch. Nothing could be left to chance. Nothing. Redundant questions and unnecessary stress, right now, would serve absolutely no purpose and might even retard the initial metamorphosis. So, Edward Stawson would keep silent vigil beside his creation for the next hour or so.

"Alex, you may recline on the examination table. Go to sleep, if you wish."

Although the excitement of the moment militated to the contrary, Alex was powerless against the deep, forceful, and protective sleep, which enveloped his being and embraced him like a mother. God only knew what he dreamt about, or what went through his head during that brief respite from reality, that brief interlude of repose. He may have even sought momentary mental and physical sustenance in the netherworld. Nothing was certain. This was virgin territory. No one knew where the path would lead. No one knew where the path would end.

Edward Stawson had been the shipbuilder, making sure the design and structure were sound. There was no doubt, however, as to who the captain would be. The waters were uncharted and the going might be rough at times, but it was of the utmost importance that Alex make this maiden voyage. The flatness of his perceived world must be converted to a full circle. He had already almost fallen off the edge. If the brave new world, to which he was about to become part, did not reveal itself round, then his descent, via a short detour to a dresser drawer and the handgun it harbored, would be short and sweet.

As Alex's two-hour, rejuvenating nap came to a close, he appeared to be somewhat disoriented to time and place. A fleeting look of terror in his eyes was not wasted on Dr. Stawson, who had expected as much.

"How are you feeling?"

"I'm burning up inside, Doc. My veins feel like they are about to explode."

"Alex, I wish I could tell you that was normal, but I really can't. I don't know if it is."

"When are you going to inject the other patients?"

"There are no other patients."

6

Reawakening

The initial, momentary trepidation, brought on by Edward Stawson's last words, passed in a flash, as did the next three months. Every Monday morning at eight-thirty a.m., like clockwork, Alex religiously received his fix of potion, otherwise known as FOY1. Every Monday morning he felt one step closer to the end of the tunnel. Was that the reality of the matter, however, or just wishful thinking? He could not know for sure, nor could the good doctor, having never fired the magic bullet before. Needless to say, Alex was at a crossroads, and, with each passing week, it became painfully obvious to him that there was no turning back, whether the elixir worked or not.

Stawson, for his part, played the keen observer. Certainly, he had grown quite fond of Alex over the last few months. This was science, however, and that meant business. Many lives would be changed, and some even saved, should FOY1 work, not to mention the substantial financial rewards to be reaped. Stawson fleetingly envisioned a Nobel Prize, a home on the French Riviera, and red carpets rolled out for him in the parlors of the highest social circles. Yes, research would have its rewards, and years of sacrifice, once thought lost in vain, would make a prince of a pauper. That is, if his guinea pig cooperated.

Over the initial three-month period, Dr.

Stawson frequently asked Alex if he saw or felt any changes in his anatomy or physiology. Alex's response was always the same. Immediately after the injections of FOY1, his arteries and veins felt as if they would burst, and a sense of profound warmth would encompass his entire corporeal surface, only to be replaced by sheer exhaustion moments later. A two-hour rejuvenating sleep and an escorted walk to the front door inevitably followed, and it was not until he heard the clicks and clacks of the elevated train tracks that he would feel capable of performing a reality check.

Edward Stawson, on the other hand, began to observe discernible changes in both the appearance and behavior of his protégé, brother-in-arms, or guinea pig, whichever term struck his fancy that particular week, or served to reinforce his delusions of grandeur. Blessed with a keen, objective, investigative eye, perhaps second only to Ramón y Cajal, Dr. Stawson went about his work with the same alacrity and sense of urgency of a mother preparing Christmas dinner for a large, extended family. He left nothing to chance.

The three months passed quickly, more like three days in retrospect, for both artist and masterpiece. Would Alex become Stawson's crowning glory, or simply a freak of manipulated nature, an experiment gone terribly wrong. Only time would tell, and yet, the seeds of a possible, fruitful future harvest had not only been planted, but had also begun to show signs of germination.

Alex Bales was, indeed, a changed man. He knew it, and so did Edward Stawson. His hair had become darker and thicker, his vision more acute, and his previous daily aches and pains had miraculously disappeared. When Alex looked into a mirror, he no longer saw the man he could have been, but rather observed a world of possibility, there for the taking. Nothing would be out of his reach now, nor would any goal be unattainable. He was young again, and his second stab at living would be tinged with the blood of those hapless victims unfortunate enough to cross his professional path. He would be ruthless in business, but his personal life would become both a joy and an inspiration, not the emotional shambles of his previous existence. This he promised. This he vowed. This he foresaw in his mind's eye.

Yes, the last three months had passed imperceptibly, and Alex and Edward were about to part company. This would be their last encounter, at least for some time. They would no longer be joined at the waist. The four-legged creature would be transformed into two bipeds. Edward Stawson desired this, and Alex Bales required this. The laws of nature, however, demanded this.

On that fateful morning, their last together, everything proceeded normally for Alex and Edward. Words were unnecessary to convey the emotions that each felt. After all, they were grown men, not babies, and they both knew the score. They had charted unknown waters together, and must do so still. Their routes, however, would diverge from this point on, and their paths might never cross again. One of them would take a shortcut, and reach his future destination directly. The other would arrive in a roundabout way, via brief sojourn in a future past.

Each was fully and painfully aware that his journey might be inevitably marred by pitfalls, and that occasional minefields might have to be traversed. Nevertheless, there would be an endgame, and results, whether they be positive or negative, would be achieved. If nothing else, the contract signed in blood between the two men stipulated this.

Although icing on the cake would most certainly be hailed as a pleasant surprise, Alex and Edward were not delusional, and good faith might be the only sine qua non in their common bag of tricks. Wariness of false gods, prophets, and promises would serve them in good stead and empower them to not let down their guards for an instant, lest starting over with a new lease on life reveal itself a non sequitur in the aftermath.

"Well, Alex, there are no fireworks or marching bands, but I guess you could say that this is your Independence Day."

"Huh, Doc? What do you mean?"

"I mean it's time for the bird to fly. You must test your wings, Alex. We must split up here, and go our separate ways. I, to continue my research and begin work on FOY2. You, to live your new life. I envy you, Alex. You will be walking on the moon, without ever leaving the Earth. I wish I could go with you."

"Does this mean we won't be seeing each other again?"

"You never know, Alex. When you least expect it. I may be there. Keep the faith. Now, get out of here. Go and enjoy your life. Summer's here, and you're a new man."

An uneasy feeling came over Alex, as Stawson led him to the front door for the last time. He was about to embark on the most important journey of his life, and he must of necessity be alone. There would be no guide or chaperone to smooth the path's rough edges. His only travel companions would be his inner demons, and God only knew, he had a few. He would look at the bright side, though. The doctor was right. Summer was truly here, and

Alex would now turn his attention and his new, finely tuned physiology to the six primal staples of twenty-first century manhood: power, money, women, travel, fast cars, and education, in that order. Nothing and no one would bar his way. No task would be too great for the product of Dr. Stawson's wizardry.

But what if there were problems? What if everything did not go as planned? What if the FOY1 concoction proved not to be an elixir, but a poison? Edward Stawson had not left him with an "out." Alex might be walking a tightrope with neither harness nor safety net below. Still worse. He may have been thrown to the lions, and that was no joke. And why had the good doctor been so cryptic? "When you least expect it, I may be there," he had said. Whew. What did that mean? As he crossed the threshold from the security of Stawson's humble dwelling to the unknown of a cruel, harsh reality, Alex's fears, reservations, doubts, and questions grew exponentially. There was no time now for pacification, clarification, or recrimination. The ball was in his court, and further explanations were out of the question. The moment to bite the proverbial bullet and run had finally come.

Alex could not help but look back at Stawson one last time, as he departed the womb. No final words would be exchanged. Alex knew that. No pat on the back would breed encouragement. Simple silence, pure, elegant. Nothing more. As the trade winds were about to whisk him away, Alex, for a split second, thought that he recognized sadness and despair in the good doctor's countenance. Perhaps he was mistaken, though. Edward Stawson, like the Rock of Gibraltar, was incapable of emotion. Firm, strong, indomitable, he would trudge onward to find new guinea pigs and new horizons. FOY2 would now become his Holy Grail, even though all the facts were not in on the FOY1 that had reached the far corners of Alex's circulatory system.

Before he knew it, Alex was back out on the street. It all seemed like such a dream. Had he ever, indeed, met Edward Stawson, or had all this been but a figment of a fertile imagination? After all, if it were possible to invent savior and magical potion, Alex would have been at the forefront of the creative process. As he crossed sidewalk cracks and gazed at gutted buildings, boarded windows, and patches of grassless earth on his not-so-merry way to the Austin Boulevard elevated train platform, Alex was smitten by a sense of revitalization and new insight. From that moment on, beggars, bankers, and thieves would pose no match for him. He now relished a rematch with the black gentlemen he had encountered on his first visit to Stawson's office.

Wait just one second, however. Alex was a mere half-block from Stawson's den of inequity, when he was nearly floored by an overbearing sensation to look back. He could not help but feel that he was being followed, but a fertile imagination might have been part and parcel of a newfound paranoia triggered by three months'-worth of FOY1. Perhaps the latter was more of a "nix-er" than an elixir. Hadn't Stawson stated repeatedly that the drug might possess untold and never before-documented side effects. Fertile terrain might not be so fertile, after all, and perhaps the fertilizer used to regrow Alex's youth was not without its toxic ramifications on mind, if not body. Fountain of youth? Bah, humbug. This was getting serious. Had he been duped? Had the last three months been an exercise in utter futility? The fact that Alex prided himself on the fact that he was not one to be fooled by cheap tricks and sleight of mental hand did not make Stawson's medical chicanery any more palatable.

As he spun around to observe whatever fate held in store for him, why was he not surprised to see a "daughter of Dracula" huffing and puffing, as she hurried to close the 200-or-so-foot-distance between herself and her bloodlust. Yes, it was Marie Comanescu hot on his tail, but what could she possibly want? In the last three months, they had hardly exchanged ten sentences, let alone niceties and cordiality. All Alex could do was brace himself for the onslaught, as she approached with full guard down.

"Mr. Bales," her two words bespoke her utter breathlessness after the pursuit, "I just had to follow you."

"What are you talking about, Ms. Comanescu?" Alex surprised that he not only remembered her Eastern European name, but had even pronounced it correctly. Perhaps there had been some progress made, after all, and subsequent to the FOY1 regimen. Give-and-take might have been, and perhaps always is, the name of the game.

"If you'll give me a moment to catch my breath and walk with you a bit, I'll explain."

"Okay. You have two minutes, but I warn you, you're neither my cup of tea nor safe harbor in my storm; even if you were the last woman on God's green earth."

"Be careful how you use that name. 'God' has certainly not done you any favors." That assertion sent a momentary chill down a spine Alex had long thought numb to emotion, physical sensation, or the weather.

"Get to the point, please. I have things to do."

"I admire you," was the simple affirmation that followed. It threw Alex for a loop, and now left him breathless. Was she kidding? Where was this going? She continued, "I'd like to spend the rest of the day with you. You're a first for me. You stood up to my master and mentor months ago, and I have never seen anyone, man or beast, do that before. You're one of a kind, and I myself could never have undergone and withstood the treatments you endured."

Alex was absolutely speechless at her verbal barrage, and more than a little troubled by the "man or beast" portion of her statement and the fact that she herself did not have the confidence in her mentor's abilities to ever undergo a similar FOY1 regimen.

"What are you trying to say, Ms. Comanescu?"

"If you'll call me Marie and allow me to spend the day with you here in Oak Park, I'll show you what you are capable of, and how you've misjudged me." This latter declaration could not but intrigue Alex. Had he, indeed, rushed to judgment on her score, or was this just another act in a subtle or not-so-subtle, passion play of existential subterfuge? All options left to him were still on the table, but his answer to her invitation would have to be forth-coming soon, as they rounded the bend from Humphrey Avenue and made their way onto Lake Street, two blocks from the Lake Street elevated train; and a thirty-minute ride to downtown Chicago and Alex's definitive break with Stawson and his one-woman menagerie.

"What do I have to lose, Marie. You've already taken my mind, body, and soul. Sure, I'll spend the rest of the day with you, but what you have to say better be good." Alex was bluffing, of course, as he was as curious as hell to learn where Stawson's storm trooper was running with this.

"My car is back there on Humphrey."

"I'd rather take a cab," was Alex's terse reply, trying to exercise what little control was left to him in a situation that might be beyond that now; and, furthermore, beyond his comprehension. To make matters worse, Marie Comanescu was not looking all together unattractive to him now. Her tight black slacks and form-fitting, white cashmere sweater accentuated her chunky, but healthy-looking, calves and an abundant bosom that promised a turbulent but nonetheless enjoyable roll in the hay.

After catching a cab at the busy intersection of Austin Boulevard and Lake Street, Alex and Marie made the short eight-minute trip to the center of the Village of Oak Park, a well-known western suburb of the City of Chicago that had long ago lost its fascination for the well-heeled crowd; but still maintained a brisk tourist trade thanks to an abundance of Frank Lloyd Wright architecture and its relative vicinity to the downtown Chicago Loop. The couple jettisoned their taxi on Oak Park Avenue, and proceeded to spend the afternoon touring small bookstores, two parks, several sidewalk cafes, and an endless series of Frank Lloyd Wright homes on North Kenilworth Avenue; all the while Alex a bit too reluctant, and perhaps scared, to boot, to ask his "female Gestapo tour guide" what the hell they were doing there. Finally, after a pair of chef salads and a bottle of California white wine for lunch, it was time to kick the conversation into high gear. In vino veritas.

"Just what are we doing here, Marie?"

"I'll be totally honest with you. I just want to know how it works."

"What works?"

"You know."

"If you're talking about Stawson's concoction, I really don't know yet. It's only been three months."

"That's not what I meant." The glint, not glare, in her eyes made translation unmistakable. The "it" Marie had referred to was that portion of Alex's anatomy that Stawson's telemetry had not been able to weigh in on. The question remained, however, as to whether Marie Comanescu was a simple data collector and extension of Edward Stawson's right hand, among other things, or whether she held an honest fascination for his plight; and, if not for the latter, then for the power, potency, and perhaps even immortality he held in his arteries and veins, as well as between his legs.

Alex came to the obvious conclusion that for whatever reason, she wanted to put him to the test, and he would let her. Should he make "it" easy for her, or should he make her work for "it?" That was the simple, and only, question that needed to be resolved. "Where do we go from here, Marie?"

"If you'll allow me to, I'll show you. You must place yourself freely, and with no preconceived notions or reservations, in my hands."

"I intend to," and Marie knew he meant it, both literally and figuratively. It was four p.m. now, and the sun had traversed the greater part of its quotidian trajectory. Marie took Alex by the hand, and they made the five-block walk from downtown Oak Park to the Oak Park Arms Hotel, a local landmark with the "arms" portion of its name not lost on Alex; who imagined hands, mouths, and other anatomical accessories also having crucial places in their future sexual, if not romantic, interlude. What Alex found strange, however, was the fact that Marie insisted on walking on the outer, street-side of their sidewalk duet, which ran countercurrent to the conventional wisdom and tradition of a couple's walk. It was as if, he thought, she wished to be in control. On several occasions during their half-mile jaunt to the hotel, when Alex tried to seize the high ground by moving to the street-side of the sidewalk, he was forcibly, yet gently, moved to its inner environs by Marie; in much the same manner that a champion Olympic speed skater vies for position.

The rest was a blur, as Alex had no recollection of checking into the Oak Park Arms Hotel. When he finally got his bearings, he realized that he was lying supine in a large, king-sized bed in a strange and ornately furnished bedroom. Ten or so, large red candles provided dim background lighting of the chamber, and, to Alex's horror, he found all of his limbs bound, but gently so, to the four bedposts. What the hell was going on? Had he been drugged? Was it possible that he had let down his guard, or were more sinister forces, beyond mortal comprehension, at play? Although not gagged, Alex would not scream or cry out. He was curious, and wished to see where the current of his River Styx would take him. As the sumptuous, naked white flesh of Marie entered the room, his fear, curiosity, and anticipation of her favors fed his erection.

"Do you know where this is going, Alex?"

"No, I don't, but I can make a guess. Just who are you, anyway?"

"Sit back, and enjoy. I'll do all the work. You'll find out soon enough who I am, and where this is going. In the meantime, as they say in transportation circles, leave the driving to me." And driving there was. Pile driving, that is.

As Alex laid back to enjoy the ride, and Marie straddled him, no verbal objections, entreaties, or sparring on his part became necessary. With a minimum of foreplay, Marie got down to the "nasty," and humped him for all he was worth. Tens of minutes went by, as Alex became more than a little surprised at his own staying power. He was more than a match for this Eastern European time bomb, and it was only a question of time before his current world would inevitably explode. His last conscious sensation before the light at the end of the tunnel extinguished itself was neither the climax of orgasm nor the pool of combined sweat he lay in, but rather the morphed countenance of Marie; which had assumed features akin to otherworldly, as its owner humped, pumped, and jumped for everything she was worth. Fear was no longer an element of Alex's rampart, as he could not help but think that a trick of the light (candlelight, that is) had played into his already overactive imagination. That was all he remembered, as he passed into the crepuscular world of dreams.

Clickity-clack and the grinding screech of steel on steel put a damper on the meanderings of Alex's mind, as he tried to determine whether his encounter with Marie had been of the third kind. Had it all been a dream? After all, when he had awoken, Marie was nowhere to be found. Her note in chicken scrawl, which read, "We'll be together again, soon enough," was evidence, at the least, of the reality of their ménage à deux, if not of future horror or exhilaration, too.

The Lake Street iron horse slowly approached the Chicago Loop. Shortly, he would be taking his place among the throngs of humanity, to sort out old cares, woes, and worries in a new body and, hopefully, with a new mindset; with the Susie, Judy, and Marie "things," nothing more than distant memories. As the Chicago River and the Merchandise Mart passed by to his left, Alex wondered whether he would view other old friends in the same light, or whether they would take on an entirely new significance and meaning for him. Would previous tones and hues cede to shades of gray, and vice versa? All this remained to be seen, and would require far more than a half-hour's introspection.

He must plot his course carefully, in minute detail. Caution might be thrown to the wind in the long run, but in the early planning stages there could be no substitute for methodical calculation. Papers would have to be drawn up, funds transferred, surrogates selected, and, above all, tracks covered. Alex needed people he could trust, if his plan was to work. And, yet, fate had snatched poor Randy, his alter ego and only chum, right out from under his nose. There could be no hesitation here, however. He knew exactly what he must do. Personnel would be jockeyed into key positions, and pounds of flesh would be paid for their complicity. It would not be easy, but it surely could be done. Then our hero could slowly fade into the sunset, not to end his days, but rather to start all over again.

That sounded like a plan. Two weeks to fill in the gaps and tie up any loose ends, and, voilà, he would set the juggernaut in motion. Alex would no longer occupy himself with earthly matters and questions of finance. He would cede the helm to a managerial staff who, for a handsome sum, would steer his corporation clear of raiders, sharks, and dangerous waters. Company profits would be channeled into his new lifestyle, as Alex sculpted a new identity for himself. It all sounded so simple. What could go wrong. Success was guaranteed.

As he slowly made his way on foot to his apartment on the Northside of Chicago, Alex took advantage of the last two blocks to come up with a working formula for the next few days. If all went well, in a matter of two weeks, maximum three, he would be able to shed his outer skin and slither away into anonymity. Telephone calls, emails, faxes, and telegrams would be the weapons employed to break the links of the chain that now bound him to Chicago. A new destination, for a new life, would have to be selected, and the sooner the better.

A smile, the first in months, began to take shape on Alex's expression-less puss, transforming his appearance from that of a Parkinsonian zombie to that of a being with some semblance of warm-bloodedness. His strange meandering off the beaten track with Marie Comanescu hours before had been an obligate rest stop, for what was to follow. It would in no way delay or hamper his staying the course. As he approached the main door of his apartment building, a distant voice momentarily interrupted his ponderings. To focus on the voice would disrupt his thought processes completely, but he was left with no choice. Alex recognized the voice as that of Sam, the owner and proprietor of his favorite neighborhood newspaper stand.

"Haven't seen you in a while, Mr. Bales."

"I've been around."

"Yeah, okay. You look good. Younger."

"I've been exercising."

"No, I mean it. You've changed. Your hair looks darker, and your skin is smoother. I'd swear that you look thirty years younger. Honest."

"Thanks for the compliment, but I can assure you that I'm the same person. Just good food, exercise, and clean living. That's all."

"C'mon, Mr. Bales. Tell me the truth. Do you expect me to believe that? Out with it. You've found the fountain of youth."

Alex did not know what to make of this. He was taken aback both by the newspaper vendor's bluntness and his reference to the "fountain of youth." Of course, the term was a common idiom, and illiterate Sam, who stood before him, certainly could not have been aware of the existence of FOY1. That was not only highly unlikely, but an out and out impossibility. And, yet, the trans-formation that had come over Alex was so undeniably obvious, that even this streetwise heathen could not help but notice it.

At that very moment, Alex made up his mind to leave the city he loved so much. He had overstayed his welcome in the City of Chicago, the place of his birth, the place of his business, the place of his home, and, most importantly, the place where he had buried his only friend. He would move on to greener pastures, but God only knew where. Dr. Stawson's magical formula had provoked such an acute change in his physique, that all of Alex's acquaintances would be quick to make the same observations and come to the same conclusions as the yellow-toothed, ink-covered cretin who dispensed philosophy and professional advice for the cost of a one-dollar newspaper.

That voice. That distant voice. It was once again parting the clouds of his thoughts, and allowing the light of reality to shine in. Alex could see the lips of the newspaper vendor moving, but the sound that he emitted was no more than a low-frequency hum. There were no words. It would take several more seconds for him to decipher the sound, and translate it into something intelligible. It was not that Alex was slow. It was just that his mind could now process much more information, and additional iotas of time, often in the order of milliseconds, were required to analyze, come to conclusions, and fit pieces of the puzzle into their respective niches in the recesses of his brain.

"Well..."

"Excuse me?" Alex found himself cutting off his inquisitor Sam's next volley of broadsides in mid-breath.

"I was going to say that I'll have whatever you've been drinking over the last few months."

"I guess I'd better be going."

Alex flipped him four quarters, two of which Sam fumbled, picked up a newspaper, and bee-lined for his apartment building, without further adieu. The exchange with the mental midget had been nothing more than an inconvenience, but an annoying one, nonetheless. He had felt like the prized stallion, overlord of the corral, yet powerless to halt the assault of a mere horsefly.

A look at the bright side, however. Perhaps the conversation had been a godsend, after all. For now, Alex had finally made up his mind. As he closed the front door behind him and kicked off his heavy wing tips, a vestige of the life he was about to leave, he realized that Chicago was about to become history. He would never again return to the Windy City. At least not for a decade or so, if he could help it. A one-way ticket and new hope for the future would become his calling cards. Alex would bury his past with those of his generation, who would most certainly reach soil well before his expiration date.

But where to go? Where to go? Islands, mountains, forests, deserts, all passed through his mind's eye. Civilization, isolation, the wild, the tame, the bustling, the boring; all considered, and all rejected, for one reason or another. Alex scrutinized the travel section of the newspaper, as if it were a treasure map. Yet he could not break the code. Somewhere in those pages lay his playground and his final resting place. But where?

After what seemed like hours, but was a mere twenty minutes, to be exact, Alex had narrowed his choices down to five. South Africa just did not seem right. Australia would be saved for still another life. Paris, ah, Paris. Well, Alex was not in the mood for love. So, Paris, too, was a nix. That left only two. For better or worse, he would spend the rest of his life between Rome and San Francisco.

Though a jetsetter, he was not, those two cultural Meccas would not only give him food for thought, but would also satisfy his wanderlust. He had been to both places before, although only briefly. Almost half a century earlier, when he had been an undergraduate at Loyola University of Chicago, Alex had spent his entire junior year abroad, at the university's overseas branch in Rome. That had been an exciting and joyous adventure, which had ended all too soon. Although the ink had long ago faded on those pages of his life, the memories were still there. All that was needed was a short refresher course, or an army of monks to transcribe new adventures in old haunts and familiar places.

San Francisco, too, had seen the light of Alex's day. While a graduate student at Berkeley in the mid- and late 70's, he had been an integral part of the vanguard of the late protest movement. At that time, when not roaming the Berkeley hills, or seeking comfort and sustenance in one of Oakland's numerous underground coffee houses, Alex could be found on Fisherman's Wharf, breathing the unadulterated ocean air and devouring the old, but still surprisingly fresh and invigorating, teachings of Burroughs and Kerouac. Ah, yes. Those were the days. And history would be repeating itself, soon enough.

A decision would have to be made, and quickly. Which would it be, Rome or San Francisco? Perhaps both. That was it, thought Alex. Both. After all, he was young again, and time was once again on his side. Why should he have to restrict himself to only one place. There was time enough for both, and he would enjoy each to its fullest. Ah, "Bella Roma." He would start there first, and, when he had, had his fill of "la dolce vita," he would hop, skip, or jump his way back to the nearest air terminal for the quickest flight to the "City by the Bay."

So, that was the plan, and not a bad one, at that. A smile, perhaps a grimace, drew the corners of his mouth quite taut, as Alex realized that he had unconsciously adhered to his most trusted tenet, "Keep it simple, stupid." or kiss. Indeed, the plan in itself was not complicated. The itinerary was not exotic, nor were the destinations strange to him. He had "been there, done that" before. The rest of his life would be nothing more than a refresher course. Alex would bring himself up to speed from the moment his feet hit the tarmac. The basic concepts were already in place, but now he would have to pay more attention to detail. He had been given a new life by an old man in one of the seedier suburbs of Chicago, and now he would play that life out on the world's stage. Not bad. Not bad at all. Obscurity would cede to fame. Fame would bring fortune, and fortune would mesh with power to harness ultimate happiness.

Alex had time, and plenty of it. He knew that the success or failure of the rest of his life depended on him, and him alone. A second chance, a reprieve, had been granted to him, and he would make the most of it. Errors would not be repeated, traps would not be fallen into, and depression would be nipped in the bud. Alex would be damn sure to avoid previous mistakes, and he would hedge his bets so that if lightning were to strike twice in the same place, he would be wearing rubber shoes.

It was all under control in his mind, and that was a good place to start. Now he would have to implement his plan, and that would take every ounce of resourcefulness in his arsenal, if he wished to proceed beyond the bottled-up beachhead of his past life. Patience would win the day, a patience he had first learned many years ago from the Romans ("i Romani") themselves. He must be methodical, and, yet, too much dawdling, in the guise of thoroughness, might not only postpone his departure, but could perhaps terminate it definitively. No, a quick surgical strike was called for. Alex must make his travel reservations the very next day, and depart immediately. The sooner he cut all ties with the past, the better.

Alex looked up at the wall clock. It was getting late. He had been lost in a pensive state, and alone with his thoughts, for many hours now. Time had flown, and he was quite tired. He would leave details and logistic concerns for the morrow. It was imperative that he get some rest. Alex had been through a helluva lot, and his batteries needed a good recharging. As he made his way to the bathroom for a quick piss, and then a wash, a brush, and a gargle, he could not help but notice that the sense of fatigue he now felt was quite different from that which he had experienced in the past. As he looked at himself in the bathroom mirror, he was surprised to see that there were no bags under his eyes, and that his skin was smoother and more vital than normal.

He chuckled to himself, "That ol' Stawson is a wizard."

It was simply a matter of seconds, after his head hit the pillow, before Alex left his past behind and steered a brave new course; at first, in a good night's dreams, but soon to follow in the real world of dog-eat-dog and thick skins. This would be fun. Equipped with a new face, a new look, a new body, and a new outlook, Alex was now in a position to follow the road less traveled at the fork. This time minus the self-doubt and insecurities common to beings who have lived but a single life.

7

Life's Little Pleasures

Life's little pleasures are often taken for granted. A stuffed animal, a vintage photograph, an old piece of clothing, can all bring extreme joy to the beholder. For others, on the contrary, something a little more dramatic must be in the cards. A walk down the aisle can be especially sweet to a wallflower who has always longed for even a misguided shot at love or a simple roll in the hay. A perfect game tastes of ambrosia and nectar to the pitcher with a consistent losing record. A new life can illuminate horizons in much the same way that a damp mop head reveals treasures heretofore buried in cobwebs molded by the hands of time. Hopefully, that would be the case for Alex's soon-to-be-hatched future, which at the moment was but a figment in the incubator of his mind.

Planning the intercontinental jump had been relatively easy, with a quick visit to the nearest travel agent. A dispensing with formalities, a getting down to business, and twenty minutes later, as painless as a cleaning at the dentist's, Alex was back out on the pavement, itinerary in hand. Actually, the logistics of his journey were much less complicated than navigation in a complex maze of stores in a crowded shopping mall. A three-hour layover in New York, a light, eight- or nine-hour sleep, and a forty-five-minute jaunt through customs would be the surmountable barriers to Alex's date with "la dolce vita in bella Italia." This time, the New World would discover the Old, and, with the help of a wizard, a medical miracle, and an open mind, from the ashes of a previous, failed existence would rise the gleaming beams and infrastructure of a work in progress, a new lease on life.

That week went by quickly, so quickly that Alex barely had enough time to complete all the preparations necessary for a clean cut of the umbilical cord. With one day remaining before departure, and few items checked off his "to do" list, he became jittery. The task at hand was daunting, and, yet, if he could just let go of all the ties that bound him and all his old ways of doing things, he knew he would win the day. Finally, at twelve midnight on the crucial day of bon voyage, Alex forced the pieces of the puzzle into their respective places. He made up his mind that there would be no further preoccupation with the amount of luggage, articles of clothing, toiletries, and all such other material encumbrances meant only to throw him off track. That was the old life. This would be the new. Alex would jettison the unnecessary, and strip down to the naked essentials. Plastic, cash, and travelers' cheques would become his truest and most trustworthy companions in the first leg of his journey and, indeed, his new life. Whatever he would need in the course of his travels and whatever he had forgotten to pack could be obtained with their help, and under their particular and universal auspices.

With that settled, preparations were abruptly terminated. There was now no need to burn the midnight oil. Everything would proceed nicely. Alex was sure of it. The only thing left to do was get a good night's sleep. Fourteen hours from now he would be airborne, and any further painstaking decisions made at this time would, most assuredly, take on a tone of inconsequentiality at that time. No, rather the current moment dictated popping the lid off the bottle of melatonin, and putting the gray matter to rest. All had been done that could be done. The planets were correctly aligned, the event was imminent, all omens were propitious, and somewhere in the City of Chicago, Dr. Edward Stawson was resting comfortably. The closest thing to a smile seen on the countenance of Alex Bales' face in decades now appeared, as both eyelids and fate were sealed. He hunkered down for what was to be his final sleep in an old familiar bed, in an old familiar place, in an old familiar city, which he had once grown to love.

He woke with a start. There was no need for an alarm clock or a clock radio. His doorbell, just then, served that purpose. Who could that be at this hour? He was expecting no visitors, he had no real friends, and, while drama had recently become his inseparable bosom buddy, there was no reason to expect a courtesy call at this early morning hour. He would ignore the doorbell's unexpected wake-up chant. Anticipation was high, and circadian rhythms were thrown completely out of whack. Adrenaline became his caffeine, as Alex jumped out of bed to retrieve the timepiece that had fallen to the floor from its niche on the nearby nightstand, animated by the quake that had rocked his body and would soon rock his world. But what time was it? Alex held the small orb in his palm, but could not focus on the big or little hands. Too much "yellow matter custard," or some such similar caked substance, along the inferior eyelid margins and medial portions of both eye sockets prevented clear focus and accommodation. A quick rub of the eyes, and presto, orientation and return to reality. It was eight a.m., and time to get the ball rolling.

Only one large suitcase and a carry-on bag would be Alex's most faithful and true, travel companions, now and most likely for some time in the future. A once over, to make sure all "necessities" were properly housed in the luggage, a hop into the shower, and one last look at his den of inequity were all that remained. Honestly, Alex was at a loss to determine where the time had gone. That morning had humbled him, and, although he was fully aware that there would be no turning back, he could not help but feel a part of himself, something very dear, about to die in order for a new life to begin. A pinch and one last look in the bathroom mirror were the final preparations for ignition and liftoff.

The reflection in the mirror left him speechless. Alex had not taken the time to scrutinize his features for quite some time. Cursory glances, every now and then, had both pacified him and assured him of the fact that Stawson had, indeed, done his job. Now, however, the moment had arrived to take a good, hard look at Dr. Frankenstein's creation. Wow! He was amazed at what he saw. Could that truly be him? If so, watch out world. Alex's gaze passed from the mirror to his wristwatch. It was now eleven-thirty a.m. Where had all the time gone? A phone call to the "captain" of the Yellow Cab was the final item on the agenda. The captain would chart the shortest course to O'Hare International Airport, and ferry Alex to his meeting with destiny, dispensing with the scenic route. Alex would now just have to remember his birthplace, the site of the life and death of his only true friend, his Chicago, the way it had been. There would be no reminiscing at this point, and certainly no tears shed. He closed the front door of his abode with a bang, and was off.

The ride to the airport was uneventful, just a cabbie named Mike making small talk about the Chicago Bulls, nothing more.

"Hell, da' Bulls are just shit without a new Jordan and Company. Ya think they'd spend a little money on some decent players. Management don't know their asses from a hole in the ground."

"Yeah," Alex caught himself replying, but his thoughts were elsewhere. He was about to break free of the womb, and something as mundane as professional basketball held neither the power nor the charm to return him to a past existence and to a world he so desperately sought to leave behind. No, he was "going mobile," as Pete Townshend had so aptly put it a little over forty years before, and neither cabbie nor divine intervention could stay the torrents of wanderlust.

"Hey, Mac, where're you off to?"

Alex imagined hearing a question formulated far off, but depth of thought precluded banal response. Why was it that little people had such a habit of unintentionally denigrating the grandeur and eloquence of events akin to the primordial spark, which had imparted soul to a boring conundrum of good ole boys named carbon, hydrogen, nitrogen, and oxygen.

A few moments passed, and then that voice again, that shameless, presumptuous, uninvited intrusion on the inner workings of the meditative mind.

"I said, Mac, where're you off to?"

It became painfully obvious to Alex that the sublime could not be sought in the bowels of a Yellow Cab.

"Just keep your eyes on the road and your mouth shut, Mike, and there's twenty extra in it for ya," was his whiplash response.

Silence, utter, unadulterated. Radiant silence ensued, and attested to the continued power of paper over the decriers of the status quo, and petulant harbingers of everyday mediocrity. The last five miles to O'Hare, therefore, covered by the Bales Shuttle to freedom, were filled by a sonic void that foreshadowed a loneliness capable of spanning two lifetimes.

Finally, the international air terminal. Before exiting the cab, Alex pressed the fare and the twenty-dollar supplement for sanity into the extended palm of the nearly loquacious cab driver. No further words were exchanged. No further words were necessary. To the cabbie, this had been just another one of dozens of eccentric, temporary wayfarers who lodge daily in his motel on four wheels. To Alex, who now breathed a sigh of relief, the twenty had been money well spent. The sanctity of cognition had remained inviolate, and he was now free to proceed on the next leg of his journey, unhindered by thoughts of what could have been a nasty beginning to the adventure.

Luggage drop-off, ticket counter, passport control, metal detectors, and arrival at gate all occurred in sequence, without a hitch. In fact, when finally airborne, Alex could barely remember the steps leading to his break with the ground. That was not because they had gone smoothly, but rather because he had passed through them like one who passes through the stages of sleep; one merging into another, the sum total vastly greater and more important than any of the individual parts. There is, indeed, something to be said for those rare individuals who live life in a trancelike, crepuscular state. They are the ones who get the big picture, who see the forest, not the trees. Whether by imposition, choice, or mere coincidence, Alex was slowly becoming one of them.

Alex had chosen a window seat. He had preferred to remain alone with his thoughts and with the wispy white, cirrus pillows at thirty-five thousand feet, upon which he might lay his head for comfort and repose. The only interruption to the joy of solitude had been a persistent flight attendant's query as to his choice of beverage. As he dozed off and reawoke repeatedly, he could not contain a sublime level of excitement that showed its head just above the cloud cover of unconsciousness. Yes, he had made the right decision, and no, there was no turning back. This was a one-way ticket to life or the grave, whichever came first.

It was now time to celebrate. A combination of FOY1 and Susie, Judy, and Marie had left an ache in his loins and between his legs that required some sating at seven miles' high. Stawson's grand plan was beginning to take shape, and his potion was now showing greater effects on Alex's mind than his body, as a reserve of hypomania welled up in him; and he knew its release lay in his "getting laid." How had he become so devil-may-care? Why was he now more willing to take a chance or a dare? God only knew, but Alex had decided months ago to leave Him out of it. As he scrutinized the jetliner's first-class cabin, it became more and more obvious to him, in the eternity of five minutes, that the only target-rich environment left safely unprotected was the mound hidden between the thighs and under the tight-fitting, blue uniform of the flight attendant who had continuously badgered him with refreshments and interrupted his golden slumbers. Her coffee and tea must now include "me," at all costs, he thought. He would not take "No" for an answer, no matter how assertive it was; although the logistics of such an enterprise were not exactly something he had practiced in his long years of boardroom maneuvering. The trio of Stawson, FOY1, and Alex's newfound, unencumbered libido would find a way, however. If not, he would have a helluva lot of explaining to do to the federal air marshal most likely lurking somewhere in the bowels of the plane's cabin, fuselage baggage area, or cockpit. So, a second takeoff was imminent, as he felt his engines rev and the bulge in the center of his pants expand.

As he begged forgiveness for stepping on the toes of the smiling and well-meaning, yet obviously perturbed, grandmother who had been enjoying family photos on an iPad she barely knew how to operate, he reached the aircraft's aisle in order to begin his pursuit of an elusive prey that every hour on the hour, until now, had been more than available. Where was a flight attendant when you needed one? In days of old, those "maids in the sky," as Alex's chums and barroom buddies had often referred to them, had always been willing to fill a passenger's needs; or was that, rather, to be "filled by a passenger" for a few kind words, a crisp hundred dollar bill or two, and some layover antics, which might have included a shopping spree and some nutritional sustenance in a five-star restaurant. Was this all bloated glory and were his buddies just embellishing their already "tall tales," to compensate for "short sticks" and constant henpecking by their unsatisfied, homely wives, or was there more to it? Alex would soon find out. In fact, if a five-minute obsession did, indeed, exist, then it might explain his now nervous search for a woman with a painted smile and no more passion than the tin wings she bore on her chest. As Alex wandered to the fore cabin, the layout of the aircraft's restrooms and galley were not wasted on him. It would be easier to accomplish the tasks at hand, in mouth, and between legs in the back of the plane, and, yet, first-class did have its perks; and perhaps his paramour would find it more enticing to straddle a "high-roller" in the perfumed confines of a first-class water closet, as the European called it.

As usual, the break with reality of Alex's mind, most likely a side effect of the glorious doctor's liquid contrivance, was sharply brought back into focus by a clearing of throat, and what appeared to be a friendly smirk.

"Lost, Young Man?" came that torrent of three words. Alex became momentarily disoriented, but not all together unsurprised, to see the beautiful green eyes, dark-brown ponytail, and blood-red lips of the object of his shy-high expedition.

"I beg your pardon?"

"You seem lost, Sir. Can I help?" was the flight attendant's perfunctory and company-approved cadence.

"It's been a long flight, and I just wanted to talk." No sense beating around the bush, Alex thought. Desperate times deserved desperate measures. He would attempt a verbal, frontal assault before hopefully attacking her "flanks" behind a closed and locked restroom door. But, oh, to be sure. Should he risk it? Would she follow his lead, or just consider him one of the too-numerous-to-count, old lechers she had, had the displeasure to meet in a career spanning close to twenty years, and coupling expansive skies with cramped quarters and falling arches. She was no "spring chicken," at 38 or so years, but she was attractive and would hold up well. Alex was certain of this, as he decided to give it the old college try in his new sexuality. "What's your name?"

"I'm sorry, Sir, I'd love to chat, but I've got to attend to other passengers." Just when he thought, however, that, that momentary flicker of "that was that" was upon him, she continued, "But if you'll go back to your seat for now, we can talk a little later."

"Okay."

She had held out more than an olive branch to him. As he strode back to his seat, nearly falling on top of "Grandma Photo" this time and disturbing a beauty sleep that had seen much better days forty years ago, the anticipation of his initiation in the Mile High Club triggered the rumblings of a high-altitude emission that held little regard for the tides, circadian rhythms, or the International Date Line. Alex's excitement could hardly be contained, as the next thirty minutes seemed like an eternity; and, when the big hand and buzzer of his timepiece tolled the bewitching hour, it was as if he was catapulted from his seat, nearly tearing "Grandma Photo" from her seatbelt in the slipstream. He negotiated the last ten feet to the fore galley in leaps and bounds, and, nearly breathless from his marathon of little more than twenty-five feet, he found himself at nearly nose length, staring into those gorgeous green eyes. They were hypnotic, to say the least, but there was something diabolical about them, too. It was as if they devoured his being with a mere look. Oh, well. Alex had asked for it. Like the good golfer he had been at some point in his yesteryear, he must follow through with both his swing and his "swinging."

"This is going to be awkward," he heard himself say, all the while feeling the gentle breeze of her breath on the right side of his neck. "My name is Alex, and while I'm not a Boy Scout by any means, I have never done this before."

"Never mind, Little Boy, I'll show you the way," as she closed and did as much as the moment permitted to hermetically seal the galley curtain. She was an old pro at this. It didn't take a PhD to see that. Alex, with all his years of experience, would never have guessed it, however. With no wedding ring on her finger, all was now fair in love and in the air. They weren't even going to the restroom. As she hopped on a counter holding a microwave oven in a corner, and spread her legs to reveal a panty-less flight path promising more than a bit of turbulence, Alex engaged his "flaps;" if only to slow the proceedings a bit.

"But I don't even know your name."

"Does it matter," she intoned, "that's not what you're here for; but if it'll make you feel any better, you can call me 'Jill'."

"Then I'll be your 'Jack,'" he whispered, "if you promise not to scream."

"I'll be a good girl. I've had some practice at this."

There was nothing more left to do than insert his member into her "friendly skies," rev up her engines by doing the slow in-and-out, and hope her landing gear would bring them both down safely. He took her fully clothed, and when the flaccidity of their post-orgasm bodies caused her to almost buckle at the knees and him to collapse, bent and exhausted, against the microwave oven, which punctuated that event with a ring; they were unable to revel in the warmth of post-coital glow. The latter was cut short by a right hand probing the closed galley curtain. When it was pulled back as tactfully as possible, under the circumstances, by Jill, to reveal "Grandma Photo," Alex fumbled to zip up. Too late.

"I only wanted a glass of water," was the old woman's knee-jerk intonation, as Alex flew by her, the smell of sex still lingering in his jetstream. As he settled back into his seat and covered his eyes with a blindfold to aid sleep and avoid embarrassment and the awkward stares from his now fully-hydrated travel companion, all he could think about was the similarity between the ecstasy he had just experienced as an inductee in the Mile High Club and a doctor-nurse role-play he had ravenously participated in back in college, eons ago.

It was difficult for Alex, in retrospect, to remember that transatlantic junket. Everything, except his airborne amplexus with Jill, if that had, indeed, been her real name, was a blur. In the crepuscular state between wakefulness and neural circuit shutdown, long-term images were not indelibly typeset in his mind. An occasional glimpse of the movie, a headset falling between his legs, an elbow from the passenger seated next to him, and a choice of dinner entrées were the only antidotes to his narcosis, and short-term, at best. Oh, well. Shortly the real games would begin, and what led up to them would certainly be unimportant. Alex was convinced that regardless of the forks in the road that had postponed his return to the Patria, he would literally be screaming "Roma Victa" at the top of his lungs in a matter of hours. So, he turned the other cheek, shifted his pillow, and settled in for a cozy respite of one hundred and eighty more minutes.

A sweet, bilingual, feminine voice interrupted his hibernation at thirty thousand feet. That, plus the acid of his stomach rising to new heights, was enough to coax him into the realization of the plane's slow descent. A feeling of sheer joy swelled up in him. The long wait was almost over. Pretty soon he would be putting his new bag of tricks to the test. New body, new face, new outlook; all to be unsheathed in Rome's arena. Now he knew the synaptic energy and knot in the throat that ancient gladiators must surely have felt before facing their opponents and the surging throngs in the Coliseum. Caution, however. The net must not be thrown, nor the trident lunged, until the turf had been thoroughly surveyed. Jill had not been a figment of Alex's fertile imagination. Her gentle pat on his ass, as he was the last passenger to de-plane, had served as a reminder. While no further words had been exchanged between them after "Grandma Photo's" untimely intrusion, he couldn't help but feel that he would be seeing Jill again.

Ah, terra firma. Rome's Leonardo Da Vinci Airport, commonly and affectionately known as Fiumicino by the traveling masses seeking temporary sustenance there, was not noted for its modern conveniences and creature features. There was no telescoping, swivel arm at the gate to inseminate the left front exit of the aircraft, and it was just as well, thought Alex. For his homecoming in the Eternal City, he preferred to touch the tarmac itself, which he would do shortly. As he descended the ladder from his silver stork, a ladder which served as a bridge between two worlds, between his past and his present and future, Alex was struck by the moment. This was his moon landing and his "one small step," not for mankind, but for himself. Touch down. Sole to pavement. Soul to paradise. He had made it. At long last, he was finally where he belonged. Alex savored the moment.

It was only a hop, skip, and a jump from the debarkation ladder, which had served as a channel of regurgitation from the bowels of the plane's fuselage, to the waiting terminal autobus, as the Italians called it. What struck Alex, aside from the putrid green color of the vehicle, was its lack of seating.

There were literally no seats in the bus, but, then again, this was Italy, and Alex knew the drill well. Standing room was par for the course, and the famous "Permesso" ("Excuse me") was the order of the day. Thank God the half-block to be covered by the bus, from plane to terminal, would involve no more than a three-minute lapse of time. A piece of cake, a drop in the bucket, and hardly sufficient to cause arches to fall, in a land where their rock-solid counterparts had stood for several thousand years. All was bearable, all was forgivable, and petty concerns would have no place in the life of Caesar. Yes, Alex, in his own small way, felt like "The Man" himself. He thought, "These must have been Caesar's sentiments upon his return to Rome from the Gallic Wars."

Rome then, like now, had been the prize; the ripe, red apple just waiting to be plucked from its ramified mother, and devoured. And although she might, sooner or later, suckle another in his place, there would most certainly never be another "apple" of a mother's eye.

Mind games and cerebral meanderings came to a sudden halt, as pistons locked, hydraulics hissed, and an automatic door parted in anticipation of Alex's expulsion from the warm bosom of public transport, and entrance into the rank-and-file of the wayward masses who would be subjected to the age-old ceremony of passport control. Alex saw it in their eyes, those unsuspecting tourists. Little did they know that their first taste of "la dolce vita," a one-hour wait in a seemingly limitless cue for a meaningless port-of-entry stamp, would set the tone for an upcoming hell in a vacation paradise. For his part, Alex would not have his feathers ruffled by Italian bureaucracy. He had been through it so many times before in a distant past. But those tourists. So fresh, so unsuspecting, so "wet behind the ears." He would enjoy this. It would make the wait bearable.

Time dragged on. The usual squabbles ensued between wealthy "fat-cats" on holiday, used to getting their way in a world of excess, and over-worked, underpaid, Italian customs officials, whose yearly wage, at best, might equal a semester's financial room and board of the average American college student. Both sides were aware of this, and were equally determined to let the other know it. As nerves wore thin and tempers began to flare, Alex passed the time thinking ahead. He had remembered that in Italy you must always be one step ahead of the game. Otherwise, defeat at the hands of the descendants of Caesar's legions was a foregone conclusion, and would make for composition of epilogue in a comedy of errors, the ink of whose introduction was still wet. So, as the bickering continued and, slowly but surely, gave way to acquiescence and resignation to fate, Alex's life support took the form of thoughts racing to find preemptive answers to the imminent questions of air terminal-to-city transport, hotel check-in, jet lag, an empty stomach, and how to spend the rest of the day.

He was so caught up in his inner sanctum, at this point, that he did not realize that he had reached the front of the line until the clearing of a throat and a gruff "Buon giorno" brought him to his senses. Alex looked up to see a pair of immigration officers, young, wet behind the ears, and more than a little put out by the fact that their hard work was but an inconvenient formality to the prospective play of these wealthy American tourists.

"Buon giorno," Alex felt both pharynx and larynx contract to squeeze those words out. Although he had once been fluent in Italian, that was many moons ago. Self-consciousness is a terrible roadblock to motivation. So, instead of pursuing a dialogue in the language of the Caesars (or, at least, of their immediate descendants), he found himself falling into, "English, please."

Cursory glances, a couple of shoulder shrugs, three rote questions, the answers to which were foregone conclusions, and the hand-stamping of a passport were all that was needed to send Alex on his merry way. Now, on to phase two. Luggage collection would not be a problem. The same could not be said for transportation to the Eternal City itself. Downtown Rome was at least forty-five minutes away, whether by taxi, bus, or train. Somehow, when metropolitan travel was designed, "as the crow flies" was not an integral part of Roman vocabulary. The short trip, therefore, could be easy or difficult, cheap or expensive, and/or scenic or ugly. As Alex was pondering any of a number of combinations thereof, he felt a tap on his right shoulder and heard the broken English of a hunter who had cornered his prey. He had been marked.

"Taxi, signore. Do you go to Rome?"

In that split second, all notions of easy, cheap, and scenic were thrown to the wind. When he turned to see a short, stocky (perhaps downright fat), and unshaven taxi driver, dressed in what could not have passed even on a public golf course, Alex knew the party was over. Maybe, however, it had just begun. An official baptism had just taken place, and Alex had now been welcomed to the rank-and-file about to be taken to the cleaners. It was just a question of euros or dollars, how much pain would ensue.

"Scusi. Excuse me, signore. Roma?"

That voice again. No need to say, "No." Persistence, to be sure, would win the day. Oh, what the heck.

"Yes. Come si chiama?"

"My name is Giacomo. My car is out front."

The eager beaver was quite adept at spouting those words and simultaneously snatching a suitcase handle in the blink of an eye.

"Whoa. Not so fast. Wait a minute. Quanto costa? How much?"

"Not much. Special price."

As Giacomo made an attempt to pull away with the suitcase treasure trove, the yank of an equal and opposite reaction brought him firmly to a halt. Giacomo knew what that meant. In the split second that sent his neurons churning, he had already formulated the answer to Alex's next question.

"Quanto costa, Giacomo?"

"Cinquanta euros. Seventy dollars. But for you, I make the special price of fifty-five dollars."

"Not so fast. Fifty-five dollars is a helluva price for a short taxi ride. I'll give you thirty for the lift."

"But, signore, the traffic, the detours, the trouble, one-way streets...not to mention my license, the taxes. Un po' di cuore. Have a little heart. Make my children happy by allowing them to continue in their private school. Did I tell you that they are straight-A students at the Salesian school near the downtown train station? They have learned so much from the priests there."

Alex knew where this was going. There could be no victory for one who would deprive young minds of the gift of education, as farcical and invented as those minds might be. Yes, Alex was now in Italy, and it was time to play by house rules.

"Okay, Giacomo. You win. Fifty-five dollars. Grand Hotel Plaza, Via del Corso. Let's go. Andiamoci subito."

With the go-ahead confirmed, Giacomo swung into high gear, motioning Alex to follow him as he made fast work of both suitcase and carry-on. It was funny just how effortless the toting of dead weight could become to the tune of American dollars. As the odd couple made for the parking lot in front of the terminal complex, Alex's thoughts took a sudden turn from the irritation at having been "stiffed" by a cabbie, to the sublime realization that even this episode might be considered one of life's little pleasures, if redimensioned, dispensed in appropriate measure, and ingested in suitable context.

As the wheat fields and open spaces on the outskirts of Rome ceded position to green grass, Italian pines, exhaust fumes, and decibel rape, Alex knew at once that he had made the right decision. This was life. This was humanity. The U.S. had been the exception to the rule. This was the rule. This was the real world.

An exchange of niceties, a slight of hand and slip of some greenbacks, tip included, and an "Arrivederci" were the final parting gestures. Giacomo reboarded his chariot and sped off, to continue his daily pursuit of the "fleecing" of unwary tourists. Alex, suitcase and carry-on in hand, stood alone in front of the massive Grand Hotel Plaza, collecting his thoughts and waiting for a doorman, a bellboy, or an idea. The adventure had begun. He was on his own, and, although all roads led to Rome, he had not the slightest inkling where the road less traveled would deposit the remainder of his life.

First things first, however. Check-in, a hot shower, a warm meal, and a soft pillow. Life's little pleasures. There would be time enough later to ponder the workings of the universe and his place in it all. Alex would begin charting unknown territory in autumn sunlight, not by starry night, the next day.

8

Learning Curve

He was awakened suddenly with a start. Although Alex could more than defend himself against sleep apnea or some such other "monster of the night," he was no match for the lumbering juggernaut that was starting to come to life outside. Indeed, the pulse of the Eternal City was tachycardic, with autos, taxis, and buses forming the corpuscles of its arteries. Highways and byways overflowed with ever-increasing numbers of four-wheeled chariots, two-wheeled "putt-putts," and blurry-eyed Romans, all with one thing in mind: getting to the afternoon with as little pain as possible, so that the rest of the day might be enjoyed as God had intended. After all, this was Rome, and the inhabitants of this dynamic, yet all too human, metropolis knew better than to assume that the Divine Plan had positioned its vibrant multitudes there to punish themselves.

Although Alex was keenly aware of the fact that the learning curve would be steep, it was nothing he couldn't handle. He would take everything in stride, and not rush it. What was not accomplished before lunch could await the morrow. Life was too precious to be squandered on petty concerns. With money in his pocket, a new youthfulness at his disposal, and nothing to lose, Alex made a formidable opponent to an adversary bent on perpetual dedication to the work ethic and assumption of responsibility. Were they to have been interviewed, fifty-five million Italians, or the entire population of the country, would have most likely agreed to adopt the same stance as Alex.

As he inserted his feet into the white, terrycloth, courtesy slippers provided by the hotel, and sashayed over to the bathroom for a quick, but rejuvenating, shower, Alex was struck by the realization that he would soon be taking his place among the other metropolitan gladiators. Adrenaline now stoked his furnace, as a sense of excitement exuded from his pores, and "O Sole Mio" from his mouth.

First things first. He was the new kid in town, and a small amount of business had to be attended to, before full immersion into the pleasures of Roman debauchery could be savored. Alex had no place to live, hang a shingle, or establish a base of operations. A hotel room and a suitcase closet would be okay for a day or two, but in the long run coziness and friendly confines would be necessary to give Stawson's work a chance of success. So, Alex would make his initial business stop that morning a well-known real estate office, or immobiliare, about four blocks or a kilometer from his hotel. It was funny how far an inquisitive mind, a little Italian, and fifty euros could go to loosening the tongue of a front deskman with a family to feed and an American cigarette habit to sate. The old adage, "Italiani, bella gente," worked just fine in times of economic prosperity, but when the screws were turned, as had occurred with Italy's decision to convert lira to euros close to twenty years before, even the most amicable of Romans could find himself or herself tongue-tied. At that point, paper, not olive oil, had become the hard currency and instant lubricator of tongue muscles and greaseless palms.

A caffè lungo and a cornetto at Giolitti's Bar, several blocks from the Roman Pantheon, and then a second refill of caffeine for further encouragement at the Tazza d'Oro Bar in the Piazza del Panteon, were all that Alex needed to set the wheels in motion and his neurons firing. The aromatic burst of coffee flavor of the second caffè would have been enough to embolden the most docile Roman legionnaire against the oncoming onslaught of Hannibal's elephants, or Alex to a forthcoming joust with a Roman immobiliare intent on extracting top dollar for the humblest of living accommodations. There was no sense diluting the caffeine with a frulatto (Italian fruit milkshake) on the way to his appointment, Alex thought. He would need every neural surge his autonomic nervous system could muster to hold his own and stake his claim. A two-bedroom, fully furnished apartment was what he wanted, and an arm and a leg were not to be ceded in the process.

As Alex approached Largo Argentina, the large, main piazza that served as a tourist attraction for its noted Roman ruins, a hub for metropolitan buses, and a center of commerce for its collection of business offices, linen and stationery shops, and language schools, he was smitten by the stark contrast between the filth of narrow Roman streets and the immaculate attire, outward appearance, and attention to detail of the average Roman pedestrian. Though canine excrement lay everywhere, on every Roman sidewalk, byway, or path, three-piece suits, high-heel shoes, silk scarves, and gold were the order of the day and preferred tender of men and women equally at home in important business meetings or in the hustle and bustle of a crowded city market. The motion of those early morning hours was further scored and choreographed to a cacophony of motor scooter snores, glib tongues, and calls of the wild. Some great, as yet unfinished, concerto was being composed in real time to govern the diurnal meanderings of urban bipeds intent on finding safe haven from Apollo's energy in unfamiliar catacombs.

Emerging from a side street into the piazza itself, Alex zeroed in on the palazzo, the sixth floor of which housed the immobiliare. A short stint on the fifth floor, after forgetting that in Italy building floors were numbered differently, with the first floor in Rome corresponding to the second floor in Chicago, for example, and he was ready to take on the gods or an obnoxious real estate agent.

"Desidera, Signore?" A woman. Why were real estate agents, the world over, always women? He might have disarmed her with his charm, if only Italian were his native tongue.

"Sto cercando un appartamento ammobiliato. Parla inglese Lei? Do you speak English?"

"Yes, I do, Signore. What kind of apartment are you looking for, and how big? We have furnished apartments for rent all over the city. Are you familiar with Rome?"

The real estate agent was much more than a little attractive in her gray business suit, and, although her green eyes and auburn-colored hair were not par for the Italian course, they were nonetheless intriguing and provocative as part of a "Mediterranean package." This was the second time he had a run-in with green eyes. This was business, however, and looks could deceive. There would be time enough later for diversion, with four down, namely, Susie, Judy, Marie, and Jill, and more to go. The new kid in town, with newfound potency surging through both his blood vessels and genitals, would find more than ample opportunity to put his visual, oral, and tactile skills to the test again in the future, when a strategic shift in priorities from roof over head to satisfaction and satiation of his senses was likely to occur in the natural order of things. Then, and only then, would Alex permit that additional foray into the proverbial candy store, this time on foreign soil. He had already tested the "waters," so to speak, in Chicago, Oak Park, and the skies over the Atlantic.

"I'm new to Rome, but I've been here before. Do you have any two-bedroom, furnished apartments for rent not too far from the Trastevere area. I'm from Chicago, and I've heard that Richard Gere used to live there, and that John Malkovich currently has an apartment there. I'd like to rent for now, but eventually I might even purchase an apartment here in Rome, that is, if you Italians are as hospitable as everyone says you are. Do you understand?"

"Certainly, Signore."

The young woman, in her late twenties, was clearly interested, and not only in the question of lodging. There was no wedding band on her finger, and the mere mention of American movie stars had aroused that indomitable Italian curiosity. It is said that every inhabitant of Rome has at one time or another passed through the gates of Cinecittà, the major Italian film studio located within city limits. But, again, this was business. So, Alex returned to the matter at hand.

"Price is no object, as long as the apartment is clean, cozy, and has a view."

"Well, Signore, we currently have nothing available in Trastevere, but we do represent an older Italian signora of means from Firenze who would like to rent her apartment in the Monteverde Nuovo zone of Roma. It is a ten-minute bus ride from Trastevere."

"How much?"

"Eight hundred euros a month, with two months' damage deposit, or anticipo, as we call it, and a minimum one-year contratto. I think the apartment would meet your needs, and you're in luck, the signora happens to be in town right now and might be persuaded to show you the apartment herself this very afternoon."

The hard sell appeared to be on, but Alex could hardly fault the young lady for trying. Real estate was just that kind of "pull all stops" profession, and, in Italy, the agent's job was simply to procure prospective tenants. The rest, whether it was negotiation, showing of property, or other eventual requests, was usually left up to the apartment owner himself or herself. So, there were no elements of surprise for Alex, nor was dramatic denouement to be anticipated.

Alex agreed to the meeting with the prospective landlord from Florence, or Firenze, as the Italians call it. There was no need to hold out. He was living in the here and now, and a small detail like a roof over one's head would hamper neither the march of time nor his appointment with destiny. The woman from Florence in Tuscany was sure to drive a hard bargain, but the stress of the deal was likely to be tempered by the innate manners and courtesy of the Florentine. So, that last nail driven into his financial coffin would proceed with all the dignity, grace, and solemnity afforded to such an auspicious occasion. Alex, for his part, had become astute and savvy to the world of plastic, spreadsheets, and financial reports over the years. When it came to money, however, he was no match for the Italians, who were just downright nasty on their own turf. They'd rape one's bank account with a smile, all the while demonstrating an economic alacrity that would have made even Shakespeare's Shylock proud. Their earthly, no-nonsense acumen was tantamount to a loan shark on a low dose of Valium. World wars and memories of swollen bellies from malnutrition and hunger pangs had honed their go-for-the-throat, dollars-and-cents attitude toward just about everything.

The appointment had been set for three that afternoon, le ore quindici, as the Italians put it. That left Alex some time to burn and some empty-stomach acid to dilute or extinguish. Translation: time for lunch. A good pranzo would make the day more palatable, so to speak, regardless of its later outcome. For a split second, he entertained the idea of inviting the real estate agent along, and then self-consciousness and unfamiliarity with the terrain precluded that philanthropical, and perhaps lecherous, notion. Today was to be a day of business, with a brief respite in an oasis of street noise, large patio umbrellas, piazzas, pizza, bruschetta, mozzarella, and Pinot Grigio.

Afternoons were always pleasant in Rome, regardless of the time of year. As long as there was sunshine, the world was in balance, and outdoor meals or snacks, spuntini as the Italians call them, were the norm. For some strange reason, the carbon monoxide of passing vehicles and the smells of granite dust and mold did wonders to enhance the appetite and the flow of digestive juices. Alex set his sights on Ivo's Pizzeria in Trastevere, and plotted a course that would take him by foot from Piazza Largo Argentina, through the open market of Campo dei Fiori, across one of the foot and thoroughfare bridges along Lungotevere, and finally into Trastevere, one of the more popular neighborhoods and dining destinations for tourists and Romans alike. The pizzeria was well-known throughout the city, and in culinary circles where "bang for buck" fueled digestive juices, as one of Rome's best. It was in close proximity to Monteverde Nuovo and the outstretched hands and upturned palms of a potentially demanding and condescending landlord, with euros on the brain.

Fortunately, there is nothing in the world like an enormous buffalo mozzarella to melt away cares, as it melts in one's mouth. As Alex cut through the white orb that fully filled the circular center of his large plate, and watched the milk literally ooze from the porous surface of the transection, his taste buds took his mind for a spin in areas far from real time. Sensorineural, hedonistic pleasures, whether they be auditory, oral, tactile, or visual, have been incorporated into man's being, for that reason, from time eternal. When the trivial and troublesome of the everyday shorts the circuits that make life worth living, pleasures of the flesh, those considered the basest and most fundamental in the animal kingdom, reroute power and obviate the need for bullets, pills, and swan dives from the highest precipice.

Nothing like a full stomach to bolster courage, either. As he paid the bill, said his "Arrivedercis," and then made a beeline for Via Arenula and the number forty-four bus stop, Alex felt ready to confront the immediate future, although the long-term still remained an incognito. He was flying a learning curve with newly mended wings and destination unknown. An aggressive push through a front door from sources unseen, and the body odor of passengers afforded standing room only in a crowded Roman bus, brought him back to the here and now. Alex was back in the mirage of the real, as the number forty-four bus wound its way up the tortuous incline of Via Dandolo. It wouldn't be long now. Just a quick pass under an ancient Roman arch, a couple of left and right turns, and a kilometer further, and Alex would be standing on the bright red "X" that adorned the city map in his left hand. He was nervous. After all, this was not his home. As he rubbed the back of his right hand across the small beads of sweat that had begun to coalesce on his brow, he chuckled for a moment. This was supposed to be a new life for him, not an incubus. What was he afraid of? Suddenly, the bus jerked to a halt, as is the way in Rome when those behemoths are whipped into subservience by their bus driver trainers, bored with the everyday and their meager recompense, and more than eager to demonstrate to the cued-up, evacuating legions who is the boss. Alex found himself on the pavement again, this time in front of a small, boarded-up cinema that gave the area an air of abandonment. There goes the neighborhood. What had he gotten himself into?

Disorientation is a terrible thing. The roar of the departing bus brought him to his senses. The entire journey, from Trastevere to his point of deposition, had taken no more than 10 minutes, and, yet, where had the time gone? Unrestrained delirium in the middle of the day. Interesting. Were he a scientist, he might find the matter provocative and worthy of further unraveling. Facing Via Paola Falconieri in a not all together non-exotic land, after a transatlantic voyage of thousands of miles and the prior ingestion of a strange potion concocted by what could have been described in earlier times as a witch doctor, wizard, sorcerer, or beguiler, was nothing short of perplexing, to say the least, and might even be said to border on the terrifying.

Mustering a resolve, however, forged on the belief that a sinking tomorrow might still be salvaged, Alex trudged up the 33-degree slope of Via Paola Falconieri. To turn back now would be downright stupid. He had already come too far now, and, in his newly molded, mid-thirty-year-old chassis, he cut a striking figure, whose outward demeanor betrayed not the fragility of the inner workings of his mind. With roving eyes momentarily transfixed on each passing numeral, and transient yet intense attention to detail, Alex stayed the course. His quest for the number forty-five address number he sought took him further and further up the hill, past row upon row of old apartment buildings and condominiums that reminded him more of Cabrini Green Apartments, tenements, and the public housing projects of Chicago than ancient or modern Rome, or any European urban center, for that matter. Boy, that real estate agent had sure taken him for a no-account, wet-behind-the-ears fool. The only redeeming qualities of the immediate zone of his trajectory were the heavenly aromas emanating from the local rosticceria. The smell of roasted chicken and olive oil-laced, oven-baked potatoes danced in his nostrils, and made the surrounding eyesore masonry and stone behemoths more visually bearable.

Out in the distance, Alex could now detect the forms of the numerals he sought. He was rapidly approaching number forty-five, and the structures coming into view were much more modern and pleasant to look at. Several images caught his attention as he found himself in front of the edifice that marked journey's end. Via Paola Falconieri number forty-five was home to a six-story building of recent construction, by Italian standards. It couldn't have been more than twenty-five to thirty years old, and its red-brick facade contrasted nicely with the green lawn, Italian pines, and variegate floral arrangements in the garden that hugged its main entrance.

Alex was a half-hour early. As he contemplated a caffeine fix and some mischief of the epicurean kind, perhaps a canolo or a large piece of tiramisu in a neighborhood bar or pasticceria, he was hailed by a familiar voice.

"Dottor Bales."

He turned to his immediate right and the source of sonorous energy, and, lo and behold, his eyes met the approach of the young female, real estate agent who had just double-parked her car in the narrow street in front of number forty-five.

"It's Mr. Bales. I'm not a doctor."

"Mi scusi, Signore."

Alex had been too quick, correcting the young lady. In his brusqueness and harsh tone, he had forgotten that in Italy, anyone and everyone with a college degree of any kind was referred to as "dottore" or "dottoressa."

"The signora has not arrived yet, but I can show you the apartment. I have the keys."

Now, Alex thought, what good would that do? After all, even if the humble lodging were to be to his taste, he could not sign a lease, or contratto, as it was called in Italian circles, until the "woman from Florence" gave her final approval. Why concern oneself, however, as he would most likely reject this abode anyway. So, perhaps there was no sense postponing the inevitable. Consenting to a cursory examination of the premises might save time and energy for all interested or disinterested parties.

"Okay. Let's go."

The foyer of the building was neither lavish nor ostentatious, but it was clean and functional, a common architectural legacy handed down from the time of Mussolini to the present day, to a portion of the Italian populace who continued to revere a cultural icon that represented the best and worst of the Italian gene pool. In its heyday, the structure in which Alex now stood must have attracted the crème de la crème or Roma bene of Roman society, with colorful marble floors no longer able to hold a sheen, wood-paneled walls, and ceilings to rival the artistry, if not the majesty, of the Pantheon.

Filing past the doorman, called a bidello, who sat in a small anteroom resembling a birdcage next to the single elevator, Alex and the real estate agent entered the latter for the slow trip to the third floor. Negotiating the door to a throwback from the time when the Otis Elevator Company built primitive, yet reliable machinery was tricky. Alex had fully expected the door to open automatically, only to find that, like everything else in Italy, it required a measure of elbow grease to budge the heavy portal to a degree sufficient to insert two passengers unscathed. As they rode up the elevator shaft in the small human container more akin to a sardine can than a modern transportation marvel, Alex became acutely aware of the fact that he did not know the name of the young woman who stood next to him and shared his five-second vertical fate. He would break the ice and warm up this Italian "popsicle" immediately. Had he been on his own turf, a push of the "Emergency Stop," a ballerina's half-pirouette, and a "backdoor entrance" would have most certainly constituted a modus operandi crafted on improvisation and a dispensing with the formalities. Don't think the idea didn't seriously cross his mind.

As the inner door of the elevator parted, and Alex pushed the outer door open to the third floor, he suddenly blurted out, "I'm sorry, but I didn't get your name."

The young woman had been so intent on freeing herself from such close quarters with a proverbial stranger, that she had not heard his query. She reached into her purse, pulled out what looked like a large skeleton key, more fit for the rusty cell door of a damp dungeon than a residence, and proceeded ten paces to an oversized welcome mat and a large, inanimate, wooden sentinel with three locks. Ah, Italy, thought Alex. The three locks were a reminder to him of the national preoccupation with protection of the "womb," otherwise known as one's abode, from the onslaught of burglars, ladri di casa. In a land where electricity was at a premium and home alarm systems were neither omnipresent nor foolproof, deadbolts, locks, and long metal rods running the entire length of small, costly "gates," so-called porte brindate, were a constant reminder of the tacit lawlessness that permeated daily Italian subsistence just under the surface and radar screens of civility and apparent civic tranquility.

A quick turn of a key, or three, rather, a jump through a hoop, and voilà, they had crossed the threshold. Alex still felt uncomfortable, however, as his original question had gone unanswered. He knew not how to address the real estate agent properly, and this was slowly becoming a source of irritation to him. If at first you don't succeed...

"I asked you before what your name is, but you didn't answer."

"I'm so sorry, Signore, I didn't hear you. I really need this commission."

Too much information. Another piece of the puzzle. Behind the polite condescension, courteous demeanor, well-dressed appearance, and air of self-assurance and authority lay a fragile young creature who was just trying to survive in the "old boys'" world of the Italy of today. God only knew why she needed the money. There had been some urgency in her tone, but not enough to give a hint to secret, debt, or emergency.

"My name is Paola Grasso, and my last name means 'fat' in Italian."

She was anything but, however. It didn't take a perspicacious investigator with a keen eye to note the contrary. Alex had undressed her in his mind from their very first encounter, and then, again, in the cramped quarters of an elevator shaft, moments before. When conscious thought had reprimanded him for animal instinct and carnal desire, it had been easy to lay the blame on testosterone, FOY1, and a biological clock whose hands had been turned back in time. There was no time now for further analysis of the matter, however. Contemplation of physiologic mechanisms would of necessity have to cede the day to the cold frankness of the business at hand. An apartment was to be judged, and roof over head was the immediate goal.

Actually, the small abode was "quaint," to say the least, for lack of a better word. The myriad of turquoise-colored tiles adorning the floor of the living room, or soggiorno, which also doubled as a dining room, sala da pranzo, contrasted nicely with the newly-painted, beige walls of the habitation. Such colors, although more apropos for a seaside villa in Ostia or Fregene, just outside of Rome, nonetheless imparted life to living quarters that might otherwise have called to mind the "so-so." A tiny kitchen, well endowed with the basic makings for an average, daily culinary existence, and a bathroom, more fit for the dimensions of a circus sideshow dwarf than an NBA monolith, were acceptable, although well below the radar of the desirable.

Alex muffled a groan when his visual yardstick, self-powered by pupillary energy, determined that bent knees from a seated position on the toilet might strike the washing machine that protruded from the wall of the narrow bathroom. No comfort even there. Not even the space for a decent newspaper read while meeting bodily obligations. My God! Where were the "creature comforts?" Wasn't a home designed to be a safe harbor in a storm? Was there not to be "no place like home?" Perhaps Alex had been too rash in departing the luxury of a Chicago condominium for the bare essentials of a "Roman holiday." This was to be a new life, but why did it have to be so difficult? The hard part, the nuts and bolts, of this novel experience, had been fine-tuned biochemically. Edward Stawson had seen to that. The rest should have been "icing on the cake." Who would have thought that something as banal as selecting new living quarters might throw a wrench into the entire operation?

As Alex endeavored to find some sort of inner solace or comfort in the face of racing thoughts and unrelenting waves of self-doubt, he continued to peruse the apartment. A long hallway, tiled in the same manner as the living room, lead from the former to a bedroom floored in parquet. The white color of the single bed, nightstand, small dresser, stand-alone closet, and walls of the bedroom were more fitting for a young princess or child than an old man in a young adult's body. Alex felt like a sissy in those slumber quarters. But wait one second. That was no way to think. An antiquated, conservative view of things might just sabotage the meticulous physical sculpting of Master Stawson and his magical brew. A new body warranted a new outlook on life. What good was the glowing, waxed sheen of a buffed exterior, if the motor sputtered instead of hummed? Alex resolved, then and there, to take the apartment, cost whatever it might.

He turned suddenly to look straight into the eyes of his needy accomplice, and said simply, "I'll take it, Paola."

"Bene, Signore," was the whispered sigh of relief to this declaration of independence from the past.

There was only one thing left to do now, and that was inspect the terrace. Not that it would make any difference. Alex had already made up his mind. The rest was mere formality. The pleasant surprise of the large terrace, spanning the entire length of the apartment, only added fuel to the fire now raging within him. It reaffirmed and reinforced the premise that he had made the right decision, and awakened an impatient yearning to sign on the dotted line immediately. Not so fast, though. Nothing ever went that smoothly in Italy. Murphy's law should have been coined by an Italian.

"Signore, I must tell you two things."

Paola's grim voice from nowhere had broken the spell. Whatever bad news was to follow could hopefully be remedied to the tune of "Benjamins."

"Okay, Signorina Grasso. Tell me."

Her body language had suddenly changed. She should have been more at ease. After all, she had just rented the apartment and earned a substantial commission. In a land, however, where ultimate power rests with the "someones" above you, lackeys do the legwork for "movers and shakers" who intervene only at the moment of propitious alignment of the planets. Veto power can be, and often is, exercised at the eleventh hour and sometimes, believe it or not, just before the ink has dried on paper.

"I cannot rent you the apartment, Signor Bales, until the owner gives me her approval. La Signora Marcucci will be here shortly. I'm sure she will like you."

"What does 'like' have to do with it? This is business."

"I'm sorry, Signore. This is Italia."

Further protest would have been fruitless at this point, and might even have been counterproductive. While the power to affirm was well beyond the reach of mere clerks or impiegati, the power to negate or decline lay firmly in their grasp. One look at the bowed head of Signorina Grasso, and her reluctance to meet his gaze, were enough for Alex to put two and two together and keep his mouth shut. There was, however, the matter of the second "thing," which she had alluded to.

"What else do you want to tell me, Signorina Grasso?"

"Oh, yes. You know, Signor Bales, that what you call your second floor in the U.S., we call our first in Italy. Technically, this apartment is on the third floor, not the fourth."

"I understand. So?"

"I just thought I should mention it. By the way, la signora should be arriving any minute."

There was nothing more to do now but await the entrance of the grande dame and illustrious landlord. As Alex and Paola sat opposite one another on the worn, but comfortable, matching, bronze-colored armchair and sofa in the middle of the living room, silence reigned for several awkward minutes. No further verbal exchanges between the two were required, warranted, or prudent at this juncture, as they could lead to neither definitive decisions nor contractual agreement. Small talk might break newly frozen ice, but Alex was not in the mood for it. He was getting more and more impatient, and he just had to get this thing over with.

At precisely three-thirty p.m., fashionably one-half hour late, but early by Italian standards, Signora Marcucci waltzed through the front door. She was a heavyset woman in her early sixties, with a plethoric face, a ruddy complexion, and dyed-red hair to match. She appeared more akin to a milkmaid or potato farmer from the flatlands of Ireland than a descendant of the Medicis or inhabitant of the rich vineyards and lush forests of the Tuscan hills.

There was no mistaking the fact that she was in control, however, and that she, and only she, was the padrona di casa.

Paola rose instinctively from the sofa and walked hurriedly over to greet Signora Marcucci in the foyer just inside the front door, leaving Alex both speechless and on his feet. The dull mumblings of words being exchanged, far too low to be clearly discernible or decipherable, were nonetheless perceived but not comprehended by Alex's jump-started auditory system and heightened sense of hearing. As Paola and Signora Marcucci entered the living room area, their countenances foreshadowed an inquisition about to begin. He braced himself.

"Signor Bales, I would like to present la Signora Marcucci. She does not speak English."

"Piacere, Signora."

Alex would try to do this in Italian, although he was in no way up to the task. His hopes for this "salvage" operation rested entirely in the hands, and on the translation skills, of Paola Grasso.

"Piacere mio," was the terse reply from Signora Marcucci.

The extremely brief, mechanical formalities over with, it was now time to get to the meat of the matter and conclude.

"I have told la Signora Marcucci that you like the apartment, Signor Bales, and she has agreed to the twelve hundred euro monthly rent and two-month anticipo..."

Signora Marcucci cut Paola short.

"É sposato Lei? Are you married, Signor Bales?" cross examined the venerable signora.

A shake of Alex's mane was enough to send lips flapping and emotions peaking, and to generate a livid exchange between the two women.

"La Signora Marcucci says that this apartment is for a married couple."

"Tell her I'll pay one year's rent in advance and whatever else she asks."

Paola passed the word. Silence. Everyone has a price. Just when the waters seemed to calm, however, the "rat-tat-tat" of an additional exchange ensued.

Paola turned toward Alex and said, "La Signora says 'Non fare casino.'"

Even in his poor Italian, the message was clear. Don't raise holy hell in that apartment, and don't make a bordello of it. Subtle, right? Alex took no offense at this. In fact, he was flattered. Perhaps Stawson had been a genius, after all, and this demonstration or warning was a tribute to his work. Imagine.

For Signora Marcucci to think even remotely that Alex was capable of such hedonism and debauchery could only be interpreted as the sincerest form of adulation to his external appearance and the skill of the mysterious doctor.

As financial scores were settled, house keys exchanged, and all involved parted company, Alex remained uncertain as to whether he would ever see the two women again. He was rock solid, however, in his belief that the banal was now over and done with, and he was ready to take his place on the learning curve, set to extrapolate.

With business over, at least temporarily, it was time for the games to begin. First and foremost on his agenda would be the bedding, not wedding, of Paola Grasso. He couldn't get her out of his mind, and, until the deed was done, he would be a restless spirit and "blue-balled," for all practical purposes. This would be tricky, however, as he vowed in this new life not to be a cad, and do all in his power to not "love 'em and leave 'em" any more. Nonetheless, Marie and Jill, and before them, Susie and Judy, had signaled a reversal in course; powered more by uncontrolled hormones and FOY1 than by good intentions and guardian angels. With that mind frame, Paola was more than fair game.

A few days later, under the pretense of requesting additional information on his newly acquired lodging, Alex telephoned Paola at work. It was she, not he, who initiated the "festivities" when she gave him her personal cellular number and indicated her availability for qualsiasi esigenza, any eventual necessity. Alex took that literally, and perhaps a bit figuratively, to mean just that; anything. He would put her to the test in a couple of days, to determine whether his imagination had run shotgun to her intentions; which, in reality, had been purely innocent and noble. On the other hand, perhaps all her innate sexuality needed was a jumpstart. After all, this was Italy, the land of repression and of young women dating "old farts," if for no other reasons than dollars, euros, position, or just a bit of experience. Paola had seemed most intent on the former, when a hefty commission on a prospective rental property had been at stake. Now, she was beyond that, and perhaps the ante could be upped a bit; if not in her mind, then in his.

When Alex phoned her private number in the evening, a couple of days later, she seemed extremely happy and enthusiastic to hear from him. It could have been his imagination, though, as every male, whether infused with FOY1 or not, is vane enough to think that he is the biggest "cock" in the henhouse; and that the females of the species spend the majority of their wakeful hours within arm's length of anticipated electronic communication. Nevertheless, Paola sounded genuinely interested, when she invited him over for dinner at her home on the Via Cassia, about 30 minutes from downtown Rome; in an area that, while surrounded by lush greenery, open spaces, and relatively clean air, was considered foreign and unattractive to the well-to-do Roman gentry who preferred central urban living and environs more biped- than motor-friendly. This was going to be an adventure, and hopefully Alex's limited Italian language skills and cultural acclimation would be up to the task. A bottle of red wine and a huge box of Perugina chocolates would be the keys to her door, if not her heart; Alex's calling card, namely his financial security, on the other hand, had already been proven to Paola, when he laid down a full year's rent, two-month damage deposit, and an immaculate and distinguished appearance in an expensive, well-pressed, three-piece suit. Paola was of the impression, if not inherent persuasion, that while clothes did not make the man, they, along with money in the bank, clean and well-trimmed fingernails, and the right men's cologne, Armani or Issey Miyake, went a long way to spreading spastic legs held in inward check by centuries of tradition, guilt, shame, and grandmothers' gossip.

As he rang the front doorbell to her first-floor apartment, after a twenty-five-minute cab ride and fifty euros in the hole to the cabbie, Alex thought to himself, "This had better be worth it. I've already dumped some serious time and currency, and the night is passing quickly." He did not know what to expect, as he heard the customary "grind" of a large deadbolt being drawn back; but when the heavy oak door was thrown open, the vision of Paola's tight jeans, long auburn hair, and large, voluptuous breasts, amply protruding and barely contained in a white silk, designer's blouse, made the trip promising, to say the least. She was a vision not only for sore eyes, but also for aching and "blue" balls that sought the promise of a warm "nest" to hatch a creature that had "flown" briefly over the Atlantic before learning to "walk" on Roman soil.

"Sei molto bella, Paola. You're beautiful tonight," was all that came to Alex, as trite as it might have sounded.

"Perché? Am I not always beautiful?" was Paola's witty and playful taunt, as she accepted the "peace" offerings of wine and chocolates that Alex hoped would pave the way for a "piece." While he hated to think of it in those terms, it was what it was.

"I hope you like what I've prepared for you tonight, Signore."

"Paola, will you please call me 'Alex.'"

"Va bene, Alex. I hope you like tortellini alla panna, a stuffed pasta dish in a white cream sauce. It was my mother's favorite, and I made it just for you." Oh, no, Alex thought. Bringing her mother into it did nothing for his imaginative visual of trampolines, trapezes, vibrators, and Paola dangling naked and an "rch" (red cunt hair) unit above his long nose and outstretched lips.

"Grazie, Paola. I'm certain it'll be just delicious." In reality, it didn't matter one damn bit how appetizing the meal might be. The main course, in Alex's mind, would "come" later, on the living room couch, boudoir floor, or kitchen countertop.

Paola went on, "For our secondo piatto, or main course, I have roasted a chicken." Little did Paola know, at that moment, that Alex's secondo piatto included a roasted chicken of another species, to be prepared by his own personal recipe.

"That sounds great, Paola. Che buono. I can hardly wait."

"Can I get you something to drink, Alex?" As she brushed past him, her more than ample breasts touched his right elbow, sending an electrical current of anticipation down his forearm to rival any produced by a funny bone contusion.

And so it went. The usual small-talk, laughter, and a bottle of red wine. With the stars aligned, and Paola's goose cooked, Alex decided to take the matter one step further, by positioning himself as close to her as reasonably possible on the living room couch, and asking, "Paola, are you seeing anyone?"

Her response was immediately forthcoming, "I had a fidanzato, a fiancée or a boyfriend, as you like to call them in America, but he was non serio, and all he wanted was to stay home and have sex." Talk about a cold shower. If anything, her words had thrown a proverbial wrench into Alex's divine plan. How would he proceed from here? How could he proceed from here? With no choice and devoid of nobler instincts and sentiments, he decided to take the immoral high ground, and resort to a maneuver that had served him in good stead in similar situations in the past. He leaned over and gave Paola a long and passionate kiss on the left side of her neck, as if to say, "I understand," but with a totally different and diametrically opposed idea in mind. Alex was such an animal. In his mind, however, he could rationalize anything with the simple, "It's all Stawson and that damn FOYI's fault."

"Is that what you want?" was Paola's verbal reflex to Alex's passionate ploy. She continued, "Wait here, then." She disappeared into her bedroom, and when she returned, it appeared that she had freshened up a bit. She was still wearing her jeans and white silk blouse, however, and it appeared that the only thing she had stripped off were her shoes. Her polished and well-pedicured toenails, however, were more than a turn-on for Alex, as he and the object of his lust assumed a horizontal and face-to-face position on the more-than-adequate living room couch.

"So," Alex thought to himself, "this is going to be one of those." He briefly reminisced over how many couches and sofas he had "christened" and "broken in," in his day. He had certainly expected more from Paola, but this was their first time together, and this was the Old Country, where traditions died hard. The Italians had been doing "it" for centuries, and who was he to question their collective conventional wisdom.

As he took her from the rear, doing it "doggie style," after a ten-minute "preliminary" of passionate kissing, which Alex had found a tad more pleasurable than he had anticipated, he realized that they were both still fully clothed. This was becoming a regular thing, he thought. Were things going to go the way they were supposed to? Did romantic, and even steamy, movies lie? Was the overpowering desire to do it and get it over with immediately, to satisfy an urge, a precursor to foreplay, romanticism, and collaborative undressing? It should have been the other way around, but nothing had been written in stone since he agreed to Stawson's experiment in the first place. As Paola climaxed and Alex continued to pump for all he was worth, he recognized the signs of one of those frustrating occasions in which he was to "come up" short and not ejaculate. The latter was in the cards, as Paola lay breathless and sobbing, and Alex rushed to judgment to condemn Stawson, FOY1, Paola, bad luck, and himself, in that order. If he had, had some FOY1 left over in the bottle and a sales receipt, he would have most assuredly returned it to the manufacturer for a refund. As it was, guesswork was not an option. Just what was going on? As Paola collapsed in his arms, and he spent countless minutes, which were to become hours, cursing his insomnia and praying for a rematch with Paola before the sun came up, he realized that his life was still, and might forever be, a mess; and that he was dragging another innocent victim down the drain with him.

Alex would give it one more chance in the week that followed, and, while location of the deed moved from living room couch to more level playing field, namely, Paola's bed, position and port of entry remained invariable and inviolate. Paola's post-coital sobbing after each act did nothing for Alex's ego or satisfaction, except perhaps for involuntarily increasing his staying power and taking his mind thousands, if not millions, of miles away during their "lovemaking." There came that moment, two weeks into their relationship or whatever one might call it, when both realized that they were getting nowhere fast. By mutual agreement, they cut it off, before Alex, in a fit of borderline rage and religious zeal, sought to literally "cut it off." Paola, for her part, would continue to seek that wealthy Italian aristocrat who would never materialize, and Alex, for his, would plot calmer and more welcoming, libidinous waters or eventually demand a full refund in blood from the man, or whatever "he" was, in Oak Park.

9

Creeping Suspicion

And so ended another chapter in the new and strange existential journey of the man who would be born again. Something as simple as renting an apartment had been a baptism of fire, as language barriers were negotiated to the tune of greenbacks, and greenbacks alone. All was well that ended well, and, yet, Alex could not help but think that Paola and Signora Marcucci had gotten the upper hand. Acceptable, yes, but upper hand, nonetheless. Oh, well, in the order of priorities, living quarters were a necessary inconvenience, not the scope of one's existence. That would follow. And regardless of the commission she had exacted, Paola, too, had suffered in the last two weeks, in her continuing and perpetual search for Prince Valiant. Now, it was time for Alex to get down to the nitty-gritty, and put Stawson's machinations further to the test. Prisoners would no longer be taken in this foray into uncharted battlefronts. With only his physiology in hand, Alex would be put to the ultimate test. Could he compete with those chronologically his minors in this new playground to his Id on foreign soil? His brief "love romp" with Paola, after all, had been a fiasco. Would inner demons continue to win the day, or would Stawson's "miracle" finally wipe the slate clean and level the playing field?

As these and other more profound, and even sinister, thoughts ran through his mind, Alex could not escape the illusion that in some way there was more to the good doctor than had met his original eye. Weeks passed in a blur of subliminal exaltation. He could not help but feel, however, that he was being followed, or at the least being used, by the man who had promised temporary rewind in a halt to fast forward, if not guaranteed immortality. On several occasions, while strolling through the Vatican gardens, sipping a caffè in the Piazza del Panteon, or getting a sketch of himself done by a local artist in Piazza Navona, Alex had more than once felt the presence of an inexplicable force on his psyche, if not on his body and entire being. Of course, he must have been imagining things, as Edward Stawson was thousands of miles away, most likely peddling his wares on some other hapless Chicago failure. Stawson was the sum total of the then of his life, and this was the now. So, Alex resolved to enjoy whatever gifts the Shaman had bequeathed to him, and go about new business with a renewed lease on life. Rome was a fruit to be plucked from the tree, and, with a little more confidence and self-esteem in his corner, Alex would be in a league with George Washington, as arbor after arbor fell to Stawson's new hatchet-man. But there was still that lingering suspicion...

The year was passing quickly. Six months had already run their course, and time was now being measured not in age lines, chapped lips, or sagging eyelids, but in a frenzy of accomplishment. Alex had not aged a day, and, as if to confirm Stawson's miracle, long and engaging stares into a bathroom mirror only served to elevate the clinical competence of the man or being who had given him the gift of perpetual youth. These last six months were among the happiest he could remember, as Alex made a host of new Italian and ex-patriot friends, wined and dined an unending bevy of nameless Italian beauties, as if there was no tomorrow, and put the Windy City completely behind him, in favor of the winds of change. He was whole again. Old friends and a gradually forgotten suicide were pushed out of sight, to the hidden recesses of his mind. It was certainly a coming of age for the young, old man, and, as in times gone by, Alex turned his thoughts to the mating ritual he had all but perfected with Susie, Judy, Marie, Jill, and Paola. He would now have to find a new woman at all costs. Not any woman, however, but a woman who would stimulate neurons and drain a surplus of testosterone that had begun to accumulate since that very first injection of FOY1. Where would he find his hapless prey, or mate? Did the perfect woman actually exist? That was certainly a dilemma. Rome was a big city, and European women were more than leery of Homo sapiens, or "un-sapien" in many cases, from across the great pond. Little did Alex know that a newfound friend of his, an American ex-patriot named Fred Kaiser, would pave the way for the flow of his creative and other juices.

Alex had met Fred at a party thrown by the U.S. Marine Corps guards at the American Embassy and Consulate in Rome. Once a month, these young, sex-starved specimens of American might threw what was described as a party, but was more akin to a Bacchanalian free-for-all, to rival those of Caligula and Nero. The Marines had done the emperors proud. Alex had often avoided these Saturday night excursions into the world of hedonistic delights, but this particular Saturday he was bored, and a little alcohol might not only be good for the soul, but, who knows, it might also do the carnal some good, too. So, hopping on his trusty steed, the Roman autobus numero forty-four, he made for Largo Argentina, a piazza in downtown Rome, five miles (and three, as the crow flies) from his apartment and two from the American Embassy. Alex would walk the two miles to the embassy and its adjoining consulate. It would do him some good, and build up a thirst for Jack Daniels and the greasy burgers that brought nostalgia to razor-shaved heads and heartburn to those, like himself, who should have known better. What harm could there be, Alex thought, in reliving the glories of forty years past, when "chugging" a quart of Boones Farm or Ripple wine, if, indeed, one could call it wine, in thirty seconds or less was tantamount to peer stardom and an elevation in the pecking order of undergraduate hero worship. Hadn't Bruce Springsteen sung about those "glory days?" Who was a born-again, basket-case, like Alex, to argue. All aboard.

Fashionably late for a party at which no one would notice, Alex assaulted the staircase leading up to the segregated living quarters of America's finest in the rear portion of the consulate. Rock music blared and the odor of distilled vomit grew more intense as each landing was negotiated, until the 3rd floor with its massive, reinforced, Italian pine portone was reached. Alex half-expected a password to be required for admittance, but he was dead wrong. The color of one's American accent, or non-accent, was the calling card that unbarred the way. A good-natured Marine corporal effortlessly opened a breach in the door, cleared a path for him, and shoved a can of warm Budweiser into his hand. All this was done with a fluidity and precision that came with two tours of duty and countless hours spent in pressing palm to aluminum can, or "metal to unsettle," in Corps jargon. Skimpily clad vixens and biceps-bloated "Rambos" circulated nonchalantly, only their sideward glances indicating a wanton desire for the obligate amplexus that would make the evening memorable, if, indeed, recalled the next day. Alex made a beeline for the bar, which was nothing more than three card tables pushed together, covered with an off-white, red wine-stained tablecloth, and literally littered with a limited assortment of half-full bottles of whatever the commissary had, had in stock. If this was any indication of the way the night was going to proceed, then Stawson's work had, indeed, been futile, and perhaps growing old wasn't so bad, after all. Wait a minute. "I am the multi-million dollar man, and the culmination of thousands of hours of painstaking research," Alex mused. If the best FOY1 could do was a return to a glorified future frat party, then sous chefs in a best case scenario might only aspire to renascent Big Mac-ology, business tycoons to entry-level Kool Aid stand-ology, and the average Joe to a slide on life's loose gravel back into the rut that had led to a Stawson injection in the first place. On the other hand, if waking up in the morning with no mental or physical aches and pains at Alex's age meant medical breakthrough and a self-stay of execution, then FOY1 had done its job. A return to mediocrity and a bit of existential boredom were a small price to pay to topple the tower of jaded cards that had been stacked against him. With the help of Edward Stawson, he had withstood an enema from Father Time, and it would take more than a pack of drunken twenty-somethings to rain on his bachelor party before its opening act.

"Mi scusi. Excuse me."

The spell was broken, and Alex half-turned into the beautiful olive skin from which that angelic utterance had emanated. She was gorgeous, with long, dark, curly hair down to her supple, if not all too abundant, breasts, and a smile to die for. Rosy red lips contrasted with a black micro-miniskirt and stiletto heels to give just enough jolt to the solar plexus to silence respiratory winds, tighten flaccid abdominal muscles, resurrect long-sepulchered sexual spirits, and swell penile veins every bit as lost and sunken as RMS Titanic had been. "I know that I know nothing," Alex thought, "but I know that I want this." He resolved then and there, in the blink of a millisecond, to not tell her his problems, to listen, to not give advice, to neither criticize nor complain, and, most importantly, to not discuss money. First things first, however. He would have to introduce himself. No small task for an elder in the body of a well-honed thirty-something.

As he made for the makeshift bar, on the tail of his well-heeled prey, Alex thought of a half dozen reasons why his action was pure folly. Yet, notwithstanding that momentary lack of balls otherwise disguised and rationalized as maturity, it was now or never. All that Stawson had put into his prodigy was now to be tested. Money had been spent, nerves had been frayed, and to not try would be tantamount to one step forward and two steps back. Alex had taken FOY1 in the first place for just such a situation. So, with his "propellers" spinning against a headwind, he did the only thing a nearly-adrift human could, and let the current take him where it would. After all, wasn't this Italy? Wasn't this Rome, where the motto, provare or try, while not forged in stone, was nonetheless a birthright of every creature abandoning ship by vagina or cesarean? He would go with the flow.

There she was. As his heart rate began to accelerate, his brow to sweat, and his knees to tremble, he felt no impulse whatsoever to turn back. Alex was committed to closing distance rapidly, and the olive-skinned beauty was now at arm's length when, by luck of the draw or curse of the powers that be, he slipped on the beer froth-coated linoleum floor and went down for the count. When he came to, seconds later, seemingly stone-chiseled, male faces peered down at him, while an uncomfortable sensation of wetness basted his backside and putrid odor of rancid hops violated his nasal passages. To make matters worse, a hasty 180 degree ocular sweep of his immediate confines confirmed his greatest fear. The lady of his dreams was nowhere to be seen.

"Are you okay, man?" a voice brought him back to the here and now. "You took a tumble," that same voice, emanating from what appeared to be a concerned jarhead, continued in a tone at once both encouraging and soothing, if that were possible from one of America's finest; who had most likely been raised on a daily dose of violent video games.

"I'm okay, I guess. Embarrassed, wet, with shit all over my back, but okay," Alex responded, as he was helped up by a pair of oversized hands and arms.

"You sure did give us a scare. They almost closed us down last month, when some broad fell down at the bar and hit her head. Fifteen stitches and a concussion, but we're still open. La dolce vita, baby, I guess." The Marine couldn't have been prouder of his bar squad's survival skills, if they had all been awarded purple hearts and congressional medals.

"Did you see that girl in the black dress at the bar?" was all that Alex was capable of thinking about in that moment of calm after the storm. "Do you know where she went?"

"What are you talking about, man?"

"There was a tanned, dark-haired girl, Italian, I think, from the looks of her, at the bar, before I fell. She's disappeared."

"I wish I could help you, man, but I didn't see her. Don't worry, though, there's a lot of fish in the sea, and it's still early." With that, the Marine took his leave, off to more fertile pastures, and Alex took to cursing his bad luck and the day he had met Stawson. Such was life, and a fair shake, poetic justice, or a comeuppance were as imaginary as unicorns, the Loch Ness monster, or the Holy Grail.

So, with his tail between his legs, Alex made a beeline for the exit, slipping and sliding, or, rather, hydroplaning might be more apropos, over a liquid linoleum plain, all the while licking his wounds and nursing ill-fortune.

"You certainly had a spill, didn't you? Si è caduto Lei." That voice. The sweet sound of a nightingale, with an accent the Caesars would have most certainly committed scores of legions to recover, and the Greeks a thousand ships to possess. There she was. Drink in hand, hardly touched, and leaning against a wall barring escape from this den of the decadent.

"I'm so embarrassed," was all that Alex could mutter. One-liners were not his forte, and, frankly, at that juncture, they would have served little purpose. He had already gone face down in the mud or suds, whichever term might be preferred, and honesty, humility, and a raising of hands over head in surrender might be the only posture left open to him. But would it work? With nothing to lose, he pursued a line of questioning that would either win the day, or send him scampering home to live still another in a series of boring twenty-four-hour chapters in the book of missed opportunities.

"My name is Alex, and I'm new to Rome. You sound Italian. Do you live here? Am I speaking too quickly?"

She smiled, and the large beauty mark or facial mole over her left upper cheek made her all the more sexy, and his task all the more difficult. He had been out of practice for far too long. Two barflies, an Eastern European storm trooper, a member in good standing of the Mile High Club, and a Roman vixen more bent on renting apartments than bending at the waist hardly constituted a sufficient practicum for the main event. Where to begin? It would not be easy, as years of past experience and sexual prowess meant little, and recent rolls in the proverbial hay employing a new, youthful chassis were mere test drives; full throttle in libidinous execution, but hardly satisfying in emotional content. His expectations for himself were high now, however, and he would do his best to meet them head-on. This would be a last-ditch effort before re-crossing an ocean and putting hand on blue steel in a faraway dresser drawer.

"I am Maria Lina. Mi chiamo Maria Lina D'Angelo. My friends call me Marilina, and, yes, I'm from Roma. Piacere."

As he received her extended hand in the performance of the obligatory handshake that Italian custom and etiquette dictated in all such encounters, Alex recalled similar tactile exchanges and made a mental note and conscious effort to grasp the opposable thumb and olive-colored digits offered to him in a firm fashion, so as not to demonstrate either frailty or superficiality. Alex was fully aware that Italians took a limp handshake as a sign of weakness and insincerity, and hers was strong and firm, without a hint of trepidation. He knew then and there that he wanted a relationship to develop and endure between them, and that she would be his, cost whatever it might. Thinking back to the words of his high school baseball coach, he remembered that there comes a time when the cheers of the crowd must be, per nature of the beast, symbiotically drowned out, and batter and pitcher move alone together, embracing one another in a waltz of competition, comradery, and one might even say, love. This was one such moment. Everything was riding on his next set of moves, on his next pitch, so to speak, and Alex, like a Hall of Famer, brought up from childhood with the cowhide in his hand, had formulated a game plan moments, days, weeks, years, and, thanks to a little old man in a suburb of Chicago, a lifetime in advance.

"I am not going to lie to you, Marilina. I think you are absolutely beautiful." His Italian was slowly coming back to him. "Se posso darti del 'tu', mi sento la necessità e la voglia di dirti che sei bellissima."

That was that. He had committed all his forces to this engagement. There were no reserves in the rear. Come what might, he had done all in his power and all that his patience would allow to conquer the "Helen" who lay before him. Ships he had not launched. A single heart was his sole emissary, to be granted safe harbor or dashed on the rocks. All would be revealed in a matter of moments. All would be won or lost in the blink of four eyes.

"You're very kind. Sei molto gentile", her terse declaration bordering on a tacitness that gave Alex little wiggle room for hope.

Small talk ensued. Things were not going in the direction he had charted, and, yet, they weren't terribly off course either. Alex was momentarily unable to determine why his life, as exemplified by this seemingly inconsequential episode and chance encounter, never quite went the route he had mapped. The road was always straight and well-paved in his mind's eye, but ended up circuitous and fraught with unpleasant surprises in the real world. The matter at hand would most likely be no different. The simple was always so complicated, and the touch of a gentle handshake was just that and only that, and in no way comparable to the salvation promised by a laying of blessed hands, an anointing with holy oil, or a dash of ash on the forehead. Alex and Marilina had touched one another's skin, nothing more, in a formal manner and in much the same way as millions and millions of friends, strangers, and loved ones did every single day. There was nothing more to it than that, and, to make an amorous mountain out of such a symbolic mole hill would have been an indication of just how rusty and tarnished Alex's love life and sentimentality had become over the years. Pretty soon he might even be seeing dead people, perceiving personal communication from voices on the radio or television, or imagining romantic interludes with every female who extended him the courtesy of a healthy handshake and a warm "hello." This was how far he had fallen, and there might be further to go. To say he craved love and a warm, beating heart to create a duet's harmony from his life's empty solo would have been an understatement, comparable to declaring Salieri needed Mozart.

Sweet sound waves brought his mind back to the here and now. "Well, Alex, it's getting late. Devo andare."

"You can't. You can't stay a little longer? We've only just met."

"No, I'm sorry I can't. Domani I'm going on vacation in the Mediterranean on a friend of mine's barca a vela, sailboat. It was nice meeting you." She turned, and that movement of her hips as she made for the portone and increased the distance between them, seemed to him to be a promise of what would never be.

Now. It was over just like that. She had left his life as smoothly and effortlessly as she had entered it. There had been no fanfares, mating calls, long good-byes, or trumpet taps. Emptiness was all that remained, and a sick feeling in the gut that it was not only time that had been lost, but one's new lease on life. To console oneself with one of the drunken hussies at the bar was not an option. That would be like trading in a Ferrari for a Mustang, or a van Gogh for a piece of cheap, Dollar Store pop art. The story of Alex's life was being constantly written and rewritten, but the ending was always the same. In it, the guy would never get the girl, superheroes would do good deeds on crack cocaine, and Walt Disney would be a spinner of half-baked yarns designed to pull the wool over eyes that knew no better than to seek happy endings in a world of woes. The twinkle and luminescence in Marilina's eyes as she departed had meant absolutely nothing. Alex knew this, as he had seen it all before. There was no promise of a future encounter. There was no hope for love's lightning striking the same place twice. Only an empty feeling and the wound of lovesickness produced not by Cupid's tipped arrow, but by Stawson's metered syringe, remained. Should he go home, or should he stay? Was there something more to be lost, if he tempted the Fates and his bad luck for one more hour or two? Three hours, eight straight vodkas, two cheap beers, and a whiskey later, he found himself seated, if one could call it that, on the curb outside the side entrance to the Marine residence and American Consulate, just around the corner from the American Embassy on Corso Venucci. Rome would never change, and neither would he. As Alex wiped the last bit of vomit and particulate matter from his crusted lips and stained kakis, a Sinatra song came to mind. He smiled as he came to the realization that not only was he a stranger in the night, but stranger than the night. There was absolutely no danger that he would get mugged at that bewitching hour, only the irritating inconvenience that he might not find a taxicab home. La dolce vita. Bah, humbug.

Fast forward.

As the golden sun negotiated Venetian blinds and left its thumbprint on a forehead wracked by demons and a throbbing headache, Alex tossed and turned, much like a fish out of water. There would be no one to throw him back, however. So, with fate sealed and sheet over head, he momentarily contemplated an additional hour or two of shut-eye. No such luck. The damage had already been done, and the best he could hope for was a stay of execution and some temporary relief by means of that mainstay of Ancient Egypt, called willow bark or Salix Alba, or more commonly, aspirin. Recollection was fuzzy, to say the least, but a black miniskirt and four-inch stiletto heels were rays of mental light that shone through. If only he had gotten a telephone number or an address to go with the last name. After all, there would most likely be a hundred D'Angelo's in Rome's cavernous white pages, and, frankly, phoning them one-by-one to find a needle in a haystack was not a thought Alex particularly relished. In a best-case scenario, first and last name, address, and telephone number would be listed clearly and innocently, to be found effortlessly. In the more likely eventuality, they would not. Why fixate on what was not to be? A jump in the shower would cauterize wounds and mental anguish, as well as give new perspective and some semblance of a joyous start to a day destined to proceed monotonously. Why had he gone to that party? Why had the salt of her vision been rubbed in his wound? Days of a future passed would be certain to follow, but, for now, warm water and Irish Spring suds would soothe tumultuous yet-to-be's.

Weeks passed in a flurry of the mundane and everyday. Alex grew stronger physically by day, and weaker mentally by night. While FOY1 had done its thing, who would have ever thought that infatuation and lovesickness would have proved to be such potent adversaries to the drug's rejuvenating and redemptive powers. Samson had once again been beguiled and shorn by the likes of a modern-day Delilah, this time Italian, and, for all practical purposes, untraceable. There would be no attempts on his part to track her down. What had slipped through his fingers, Alex would let slide. The quotidian would become his faithful companion, and his early morning trips to the local marketplace, his afternoon jaunts to the gym, and his evening trysts with pizza and a pasta plate called La Carbonara in some local Roman dive off the beaten track would give his life a regularity and his mind some solace; if not the wonder and excitement promised by a mysterious and beautiful woman, an unfolding saga, and a magical elixir. Young, strong, and virile again Alex was, but living life for the second time was not all that he had envisioned it to be. His gnome and mentor, the good Dr. Stawson, may have taken him for a ride, after all. As one day followed another, Alex became more and more cognizant of the utter failure of Stawson's experiment. Each passing twenty-four hours brought him closer and closer to a fateful return trip across the great pond and that appointment with blue steel in a dresser drawer. How could he have fallen so low? How could science have been so cruel?

Then it happened. Maybe there was some grand design, after all, and perhaps the free-love, drug culture of the sixties and early seventies had not been too far off, with "You get what you need." Whatever explanation surfaced or sufficed was not important. What did matter was that at six-thirty p.m. on a day that had been no different from the countless before it, and one that promised nothing earth-shattering from those to follow, Alex's front doorbell rang, one time and then a brief burst to follow. Its sound said nothing and everything, as if, "This is your last chance. Get to the door. Don't blow it."

Alex could hardly believe his eyes, as he peered through the peephole in the portone and was struck by a vision that sired a Phoenix from his ashes. It was she. He threw open the door, their eyes met, and a single sentence, or was it the most beautiful Aria he had ever heard, emanated from her ruby lips.

"Io dormo qui. I sleep here tonight," was akin to a soft, sweet rustle in the spring wind.

Was it good fortune, a trick of the light, a dream, or were the Fates at their old games again? Alex was somewhere between elation and incredulity, as he imagined himself speaking the words, "Accommodati. Make yourself at home."

Who was the spider, and who was the fly, now? As Marilina crossed the threshold of his humble abode, a thousand thoughts, and perhaps as many impulses, raced through his mind. There was so much to ask. He was so curious, and, yet, a wrong move, a misplaced gesture, a misspoken word, or even inaction or social clumsiness might spell disaster and blow it all. It was his home, he was in control, and, yet, this couldn't be further from the truth. To win the day would require steady nerves and at least a semblance of steeled control. Alex motioned Marilina to the living room or soggiorno, where he would set out to learn all that he could about her. What had she meant by her, "Io dormo qui"? How had she found him, or, more importantly, why had she found him? Was their mutual attraction an innocent mating ritual, or was something more sinister at play? Nothing was self-evident at that point, and end-results might just as well have been written in tea leaves.

They faced each other, armchair to sofa, squaring off in a sexually-charged, intellectual chess match promising no foreplay, but rather a no-nonsense cutting to the chase. While "meat" of the matter, in all senses of the word, might come later on, now was the time for simple sincerity, a spilling of guts, and an opening of hearts. Alex went first.

"Benvenuta. How did you find me?"

With Italy being the matriarchy that it is, Alex did not expect Marilina to miss a beat, and, yet, the blush in her face said it all. She was unprepared for his question, and downright embarrassed to answer it. As she twisted and turned from her once prim and now obviously inefficacious posturing and command of the sofa's high ground, it perturbed Alex a bit that his query was not one she had anticipated on initial conversational foray. He was all ears at that moment, even though the whole truth might come at a premium. Sentimental thrust and parry had never been something Alex relished, and this was no time for emotional sway. Only old-fashioned truth would win the day, and defray the mental cost of countless hours of self-reflection, self-doubt, and self-flagellation. While the long road to paranoid schizophrenia might be lined with transitory waystations of lucidity, unnecessary travel could be averted by symbiotic stabs at coproductive truth.

"Non so dove iniziare. I don't know where to begin," she finally spoke. "I'm embarrassed, and, yet, Signore, I have to be here."

"Please call me Alex."

"Va bene, Alex. We have a mutual friend. I will not tell you who he is, but it was he who gave me your address."

From the lines of her countenance, it became clear that no amount of prying or verbal calisthenics would dislodge a revelation perhaps better left unsaid. After all, the important thing was that she was there, on his turf and at his arm's length. Nothing else mattered, not the stars, not the state of the world, not even his soul, which he had nonetheless bartered off long ago to Stawson in his existential garage sale. Funny how love can dull even the keenest of depressions. Life had thus far been a cesspool of missed opportunities, ill-conceived notions, and erroneous choices for Alex; with its second lease now, in the most romantic of backdrops in the Eternal City, promising little to blot the indelibility of passionless inevitability on an already fragile psyche. Where was this going to go? Who would dictate his moves? Was he to be the captain of his fate, or had Stawson, in some diabolical and as yet unclear and unrevealed plan or maneuver, commandeered his cytoplasm, protoplasm, and DNA via FOY1, in order to wrest self-determination from his hands? Alex was a dupe, a mere pawn in a calculated series of moves and countermoves that left nothing to chance. But wait a minute. This was ridiculous. A step back was all that was called for. It suddenly became painfully transparent to him that his mind's terrible tricks had pushed him into a corner. So much so that he was now reading too much into random human actions. There was no sinister scheme in the works. He had to convince himself of this. Perhaps he should just follow the current, and see where all this would take him.

Alex cleared his throat and erased a slate of concern. "Very well, then, Marilina. It's unimportant what actually brought us together. What matters to me now is that you're here. Can I get you something to drink?"

How banal and awkward that last query must have sounded, in the face of overpowering sentiments and emotions that bordered on total madness and surrender. Alex knew that she was the one. Pursuing his prey clinically and patiently, however, might prove to be an undertaking that he was ill-equipped to broker, negotiate, or conclude. In life, he thought, there are things that one desires so badly, that selfish passion and reckless abandon cloud the clarity and selflessness of the paths we are born onto as babes. Alex was so overwhelmed and consumed by his desire for Marilina that he could taste her in his mind, if not on his lips. Yet, in the culture of this, his new adopted land, one false and uninformed move might spell dysthymic disaster. He must tread lightly, but would that be possible? She had come to him, and she was there for the taking. Damn the mysterious circumstances of her appearance on his doorstep. Damn Stawson and his misguided potion with no instruction manual. She would be his, cost whatever it might cost.

They spoke for hours. One train of thought led to another. One line of questioning unexpectedly unbarring the path to a mother lode of personal information, which Alex would bank jealously in the protective recesses of his mind's vault. It was all there. It was all laid out before him. Yet, it was too good to be true. Nothing is free in this world, a mantra by which he had here-tofore navigated life's challenges and inconsistencies, large and small. Good fortune had, however, fallen into his lap, and perhaps ghosts, gift horses, unicorns, the Yeti, and freebies did exist, after all. His was not to question why, as Marilina took her leave to go to the bathroom to "farmi più comoda" and make herself more comfortable. This promised to be a night of intense and relentless passion. Strange, to say the least, but no less desirable for its unorthodox denouement. As the plot unfolded and Marilina retired silently to the bowels of his sleeping chamber, Alex remained glued to his armchair. In what should have been his most glorious night of ardor and amplexus, in God knew how many years, and notwithstanding his recent trysts with the "Gang of Five," as he had come to refer fondly to Susie, Judy, Marie, Jill, and Paola, he was filled with a trepidation and foreboding restraint that defied explanation. Was this really happening, or was it a delusional heyday preemptive to some-thing bigger? Creeping suspicion had set in, and neither man nor beast was immune to its free reign.

10

Training Wheels

The night had been long. The night had been too short. Exciting, yes, but draining on wits, if not on stamina. Alex had held up well to the test, performing feats of sexual prowess that had long ago been relegated to the ranks of attic trunks and cellar cobwebs. The "Gang of Five" had been mere sparring matches on the road to this main event. His heart and mind, this time, had both been in it. He had been right. She was breathtaking in her gown of olive skin. The Creator had been good to her, and every symmetrical crease, curve, nook, cranny, or angulation of head, torso, or pelvis bespoke perfection. So taken was he by appearance alone, that he had long ago forgotten the small talk leading up to culmination, as he lay awake for a good part of the night gazing at the play of lunar light on silky facial features tamed by love's acrobatics and tinted by its glow. Every now and then, Alex felt Marilina's dark gaze into the recesses of his orbits, but perhaps it had only been his imagination. At this point, he could be sure of nothing, and the morning movements in this concerto of the awkward and the sublime would most assuredly do little to dampen the cacophony of sights and sounds accompanying Marilina's approaching awakening. He dreaded the latter every bit as much as those that had preceded it in his college days and young adult life, and those that would inevitably postdate it on the short, rapid road to destruction, should dawn's early light send Marilina scampering for the exit or politely bidding a final adieu.

There was a warmth inside him that he had not felt for years. Why had a chance encounter in what amounted to a Marine barracks and a slip and fall into embarrassment been so good to him? As he foresaw years of unencumbered bliss in her arms and between her legs, Alex was nonetheless troubled by a recurring sensation of impending catastrophe. Why is the human condition such that when things are going right, we ponder the inevitability of derailment? It's as if true joy must come with consequences of some kind, in order to balance the existential scale of positive and negative forces. For every action, there is an equal and opposite reaction. For every reward, someone must be taken to the cleaner. For every ride on the winds of pacification that bellow inner peace and tranquility, there is an underlying angst that transports us back to earthly station from our perch among the stars and our brief sojourn among the hosts calling heaven home. Alex thought for a moment, only children have the luxury of a carefree existence. Rich or poor, devoid of all of life's presumptions, they enjoy the best of what humanity and the human condition have to offer, minus the associated guilt and financial responsibility. Oh, to be a child again. A stir. Marilina was in motion. It would not be long now until explanations would be as difficult to elicit and perhaps as painful to tolerate as the extraction of a third molar. Brace himself was all that Alex could do, and hope for the best.

"Are you awake?" he heard himself whisper.

With dorsum pressed to his chest, he was in the unenviable position of speaking, rather, spilling his guts, to a perceived soul mate, without the benefits of the positive reinforcement and visual cues that eyes, lips, and cheeks impart to an otherwise lifeless soliloquy.

There was no immediate response, and then, "Yes, I am. Che ora è? What time is it?"

Who would have ever guessed that something as mundane as the time could evoke an afterglow, when purred by dew-drop lips and a voice beyond sweet to the listener. Alex could not help himself. He had been conquered in the first round, and it was all he could do to grab the ropes or bedpost before going down for the count; a count to which he would succumb over the long haul and make no bones about.

"It's eight o'clock. What would you like to do today?"

It was Saturday, the day was young, and promise had shown its face on the horizon hours before.

"Vorrei un caffè, per favore. A coffee would be nice, first."

"Would you like to go to a pasticceria for a cornetto and un bel caffè?" Alex queried, grateful for the fact that the conversation was moving in the direction of the commonplace and platonic, and away from the awkwardness of explanation, excuses, and cat-and-mouse exchanges for the previous night's festivities.

"That would be nice. Let's get into the shower."

There would be time enough to analyze and reanalyze, when alone with his thoughts and devoid of present company. For now, however, it was to be an espresso, a breakfast pasta, and perhaps a stroll to the neighborhood market for the rich aromas, odors, and smells of aged prosciutto, fresh fish, and handpicked flowers, respectively. Multicolored carnations would be in full bloom, and strawberries were currently in season. Alex's newfound libido would certainly put the latter to good use, along with a bottle of Grand Marnier or Moët & Chandon, for good measure. A rub of the spirits on abdomen or, better, elsewhere, along with a strawberry strategically placed, would set in motion a chain reaction of eroticism destined to repeat itself endlessly in a closed loop over the years, or at least until physiology warranted another dose of FOY1. Alex could also take it slowly, and diverge toward the moral high ground of a stroll in the park, with its light banter, the sounds of small children and animals, and a forgoing of sins of the flesh for a return to nature and a demonstration of good intentions. These and a veritable potpourri of other thoughts, insights, and misgivings graced his overworked cerebral circuitry, as shower water dripped from his forehead onto the small of the back he was coating with lather before him. Better to take it slow for now. There would be years to put his every whim and fetish to the test.

Out the main entrance they went, hand in hand, greeting the building's portiere, whose wink to Alex was tantamount to a thumb's up, as they crossed the threshold in reverse. Destination was unknown, but that mattered little, as they had each other, and Rome's golden sun promised to smooth over any rough edges that threatened to cut the cord that joined them at the waist.

This and other similar chains of events would go on for three years without a glitch, throughout their travels near and far. Rome, Naples, Pompeii, Capri, Perugia, Florence, Bologna, Siena, Pisa, Lucca, Verona, Modena, Turin, Milan, Genoa, and Venice, one after another, they all fell in order, with Alex and Marilina cruising their streets, piazzas, parks, and gardens, arms around one another for all to see, as if in mortal embrace. On more than one occasion, an elderly couple would smile at them and comment under their breaths at how much in love they appeared to be. When the domestic playgrounds dried up, it was off to Geneva, Monte Carlo, Paris, Cannes, Ibiza, Marbella, Barcelona, Madrid, Lisbon, Gibraltar, and even Tangiers and Casablanca. They spared neither expense nor international borders, as they hopped around like proverbial jetsetters, minus the pretenses of "keeping up with the Joneses." Major problems, travelwise or otherwise, were nonexistent, as their love for each other grew by day and was proven all night. A minor inconvenience, here and there, every now and then, put neither damper nor lid on their wanderlust or wandering fingers. A slight case of indigestion in Athens, being chased through the Blue Mosque in Istanbul by a rabid band of Turkish merchants, a pinch of Marilina's derrière by a Turkish adolescent in Ephesus, and an altercation with a house servant at a reception in an up-and-coming, professional opera tenor's home in Modena all made for departures from the tedium of the status quo, and helped build the foundation of that library of memories that solidifies a couple's bond and renews devotion to one another.

Never once in all the years that passed did Alex question her loyalty, or ask her about past partners. Yes, he was dying to know, but, with the checkered past he himself harbored, not to mention the inexplicability of the man or being named Stawson, he felt that it would be unfair and inappropriate to apply a double standard by posing questions of a gander that had not also been explicitly queried of the goose himself. While Alex may have been a misogynist from time to time in his life, a sexist he was not, as he had always been fair to the fairer sex. He was not about to cast suspicion, doubt, and innuendo on this angel. He vowed that his relationship with Marilina would, from this day forward, be one of unilateral, if not mutual, trust on his part. Everything but past loves, losses, and sentimentality would be fair game in their daily conversations. This was a new beginning for Alex, in much the same way as his laboratory existence à la Stawson or à la mode, but required an entirely different methodology and new tools of the trade. He had jettisoned the training wheels that bound him, in favor of new wings that allowed him to soar to new heights, far above the misery of a past life not well spent. In essence, his maiden voyage or solo flight, if you will, was as doomed to failure or marked for success as that of other great beginners, the one most readily coming to mind being the RMS Titanic. He derived new meaning from Pete

Townshend's "Going Mobile," by cutting "The Ties That Bind," referred to by Bruce Springsteen, in an attempt to take life and love to new heights.

There was never to be a dull or cruel moment in their lives together, for Alex and Marilina. That was the plan, at least. There is an old Italian expression, however, that states, Scopa nuova, spazza bene, or "A new broom sweeps well," to refer to a new government, a new housemaid, or a new significant other all performing marvelously at inauguration, only to return to past bad habits with the passing of time. In America, its verbalization intones the "You can't teach an old dog new tricks" philosophy, and the fact that the saying exists in more languages than one is still another indication of the artificiality and utter uselessness of international borders, boundaries, and national origins, which are time and time again transcended by the human condition and human nature. Alex was that new car, brand spanking new out of the showroom, but there was no guarantee that the gleam of his finish would stand the years and the test of time. Alex knew this, but he was unsure if the love of his life would be up to speed on that score.

No children were on the horizon, as he was too content with his new-found sexual liberation to take on the reigns of responsibility, and Marilina was all too happy to be along for the ride. When brief respites in their travel itineraries left room for self-reflection and deeper rumination, Marilina became growingly aware of a slowly unbridling desire for motherhood. And why not? Three years had passed, and she loved Alex. What could be more logical than having his child? That was not to be, however. She knew Alex would not have it. The tenor of his life was just too frantic and fast-paced to warrant a change of tires or change of diapers in maternity's pit. Little did they both know that the camel's back was about to be broken, and that a failure to consummate their union and love, in the form of the pitter-patter of little feet, or a stork's nosedive, would drive a molten wedge between two hearts joined by a space-filling salve of mutual admiration and affection. That was the way of the world, with life imitating art this time around, instead of vice versa. Matters weren't helped any, either, by Alex's creeping suspicions and paranoia that everything between them was too good to be true, that Marilina was in some way a plant, and that he could go nowhere without being followed. Pure fantasy was always Marilina's gentle rebuke, when Alex found quiet moments in a chain of otherwise vibrant days, to voice his unsubstantiated worries and impressions. Marilina would explain away his thoughts and strange, but benevolent, machinations to herself as the rumblings of a dormant, human volcano too exuberant to contain, and yet held in check by the laws of man and physiology, if not those of nature. To Marilina, Alex's frequent and unpredictable bouts with his own self-identity and super-ego were nothing more than a traveler's wayward progress on the existential road of discovery, as to why his life should be so good. Nothing more.

And so, life went on, and it was good. Sure, there were ups and downs. There always are, as perennial rosiness is the stuff of children's books and bedtime stories, not the meat and potatoes of our short time on earth. Alex knew this, and was content to grow even more in love with the apple of his desire, albeit with certain reservations. What he didn't realize was that Marilina was growing more and more disillusioned with his behavior, if not his attitude and lease on life. As the next three years passed more slowly than the first three, he would spend many hours in front of the TV screen, watching the same old movies tens of times, and paying scarce attention to the warm body and voiced opinions emanating from a position on the sofa next to his. He would not shave for days at a time, claiming that he was on an extended leave and that vacations were the boon of unkempt men. He would sometimes stare at a wall, oblivious to Marilina and his surroundings, as if transfixed by an object invisible to the mortal eye, or paralyzed by a telltale heart no less potent than that construed by the imagination of Edgar Allan Poe. One thing became ever more clear, and that was the growing difficulty Marilina encountered in getting through to him, whether that be verbally, by gesture, or by amplexus. While he had never been antisocial in the first three years she had known him, Alex was now retreating behind a wall of television waves and locked doors. One afternoon, in fact, when Marilina's mother came to his front door looking for her daughter to go shopping, not only did he ungraciously refuse to open the door to greet her, but his unceremonious "Vattene. Go find your daughter somewhere else," had an effect comparable to a cold shower on a hibernating bear or incubating chick egg. Marilina would never forgive him for that outrage, and often reminded him of it; and their once-indomitable relationship descended the slippery slope of malcontent on the way to either rupture or drastic measures to reverse course. The true pity was, as is usually the case in episodes of domestic abuse, that Alex was completely unaware of the damage he was provoking at every turn. To him, he was the victim, a lost expatriate in a sea of infidels and strangers who could not understand him, his background, his losses, and the strange substance that had coursed through his veins, and might even now be stored in some fat deposit, muscle, tissue, nerve ending, or synapse of his physical or mental being.

Marilina noted a frustration in Alex, but was thankful that aggression was not its aftermath, at least not in her presence. One afternoon she returned to Alex's apartment with the vegetables she had purchased at the neighborhood market. As she turned the key to open the front door and enter the vestibule of his apartment, she was met by the unusual, unearthly sounds of silence. Not even a breath of televised white noise had greeted her arrival. Penetrating deeper into the bowels of his abode, Marilina found him bowed over, on the bathroom floor. The object of his attention was the lifeless, four-legged creature, otherwise known as a Siamese cat, named Sheila, which he had given to her as a gift and symbol of his love only a matter of months before. He was administering what amounted to chest compressions and respirations, although not exactly mouth-to-mouth, to the limp, tongue-protruding form. Tears streamed down his cheeks, as he sobbed and repeated in a broken voice the litany that every person and creature on this God-scorched earth has dignity. They could steal your money. They could deprive you of reputation. They could demote you in the proverbial pecking order or even take your life, but the one thing they could not touch, come hell, high water, or delinquent credit card accounts, was your dignity. In a state of depression, followed by a fit of rage, Alex had, for no good reason, kicked the inquisitive feline with such force and simultaneous lack of remorse that he had broken ribs, severed intercostal arteries, and punctured lungs, all in the name of feeling sorry for himself. When Marilina asked him what had happened, all he could muster was a lame, "Can't you see I'm trying to save the cat? Poor Sheila."

Marilina could never have fathomed what was truly taking place here. It was much more than a temper tantrum, a collapse, or a break with reality. Although Alex did not know it as yet, the unseen talons of lurking suspicion embedded in the flesh of his being preannounced some heretofore unknown side effects of FOY1 on psyche and physiology. This would have been unimaginable and incomprehensible to Marilina, and Alex himself would have refused to lend credence to it, until now. Sudden flashes of forethought and afterthought, to days of future past and passed, respectively, brought Stawson to his mind's eye. Would the good doctor have ever revealed the downside of his concoction to the guinea pig, had such information been firmly rooted in the annals of his statistical data? After all, Alex couldn't fault Stawson for withholding alarm on the basis of mere supposition alone. On the other hand, he remembered the venerable, if not all together uncomplicated and un-equivocal, researcher having once said that FOY1 had never been fully tested. That revelation had been forthcoming in the middle of a discourse on the presumed rejuvenating effects of the drug on mind and body. Way back when, when Stawson's indecent proposal was first set to ear, Alex's enthusiasm for a new lease on life could never have been curbed. All that had changed now, as the notion that a fluid from some as yet unrevealed fountain of youth might prolong a human body's inherent expiration date beyond twenty-two thousand days and twenty-two thousand nights was beginning to show telltale signs of too good to be true. Once a believer, Alex and the inner convictions he held in a majority of one were slowly but surely being relegated to ranks currently occupied by subjects professing alien abductions, the infallibility of the Mayan calendar, and the lone-shooter theory of the Kennedy assassination.

It took no Albert Einstein or Nikola Tesla to discern that something was amiss. Chinks in the lovebirds' armor and amour, at one time as unrecogniz-able as the solution to the Riddle of the Sphinx, were now becoming all too evident. Recalling those days when he fancied himself a poet, and put life's trials and tribulations, great and small, to paper, Alex found himself making more and more return trips on what he defined as a perpetual "mental treadmill." He had even composed verse to inform and instruct the imaginary uninitiated, as well as exorcise his own self-renewing demons. It had gone something like this:

Antiseptic lights,
Coke machine,
Door half open,
In between.
Necktie hanging,
Verdict in,
Formality coming,
Mortal sin.
Don't pass judgment,
Go with flow,
Give rote answers,
Stay in tow.
End result,
Foregone display,

Tail in hand,
Curse the day.
Existential roulette,
Spin the wheel,
Square one mugging,
Saps all zeal.

The die had been cast, and there was no turning back now. While his mind told Alex that he must salvage his relationship with Marilina at all costs, lurking demons knew better. Whether to blame the downward spiral of both his emotional and professional lives on simple drug side effect or something more was irrelevant at this point. The ballast in his tumultuous Titanic-like descent threatened to not only to strand him on the bottom with no hope of salvation, but also to take the innocents around him under. It was just not fair, but there was not a damn thing he could do about it. Plead as she would for him to get some professional help, Marilina found all of her entreaties falling on deaf ear. Was this the man she had found so adorable on the slick and filthy floor of a Marine Corps' barracks during that fateful party six years before? Was this the man from a far-off land who had appeared so sincere and docile at first glance, only to degenerate into God knew what? There were times when she actually began to fear for her own life, and his, too. She knew he owned a pistol, a German Luger, which had been a relic from an epoch long-since passed of Fascist Italy. Actually, he had purchased it from a shady character in one of those out-of-the-way stalls, far off the beaten track of the usual array of tents and stands that populated the Sunday, Porta Portese flea market in Rome's central environs. In running countercurrent to Italian law, he had acquired it from a slick operator who muttered the kind of Italian that was not taught or spoken in school, street, home, or acceptable social circles, but rather in the backrooms of establishments that boasted no reason to exist other than to balance the forces of good. Alex had literally carved a niche in his bedroom closet wall to nest his arma da fuoco or handgun. Marilina knew where it was, and envisioned a day when it would draw a bead on her heart, the way Cupid's arrow had, in happier times not long passed.

"What is happening to us?" Marilina would ask incredulously.

"What are you talking about?" was always the terse reply.

Exchanges of that nature were revisited weekly, with no solution or resolution in sight. Then, in a moment of calm in a perpetual storm, Alex would permit a glimpse into a mind fractured and troubled by two lifetimes' worth of stress, which a change of molecular structure, engineered perhaps by the devil himself in the form of Edward Stawson, was ill-equipped to disassemble and dissipate.

"I do believe in God, Amore."

"Where did that come from, Alex?" was Marilina's tremulous response.

"There was a time when I thought the Almighty had made me the standard-bearer of the flame of genius. I was convinced that I had it all and could do it all."

"And?"

"Boy, was I wrong."

"What do you mean?"

"I mean that any genius I've ever possessed has always been cloaked in depression and misery. I am not a happy man, Marilina, and all I can do for you is bring you hurt. God knows, you don't deserve that."

"But what can I do to help?"

"It's too late for that, Amore. Maybe the best thing I can do for both of us is make that one-way trip to the closet."

"Don't even talk like that. You're scaring me. I'm here to help. Won't you let me? Ti amo disperatamente."

"Sometimes that's just not enough. There are forces at play here, Marilina, that you could never comprehend. Capisci?"

"No, Alex, I don't. What I do know is that I'd follow you to the gates of hell itself, if I thought it would make a difference."

"You may have to, Darling, and what's worse, you may have to enter, too. What am I talking about? I've already put you through hell, if not into hell, for the rest of your remaining days. What I do is indelible, and, long after I'm gone, you'll be paying the Piper or someone far more sinister."

"What are you talking about, Alex? What does that mean? I don't understand you anymore."

Nothing more would be forthcoming from him. He retreated into that reptilian shell that neither words nor the elements could pry open. It was, "Damn the torpedoes, full speed ahead," and, frankly, who could have given a damn, certainly not Alex, about who or what was caught in the undertow. This was no longer about his survival. He had foregone that conclusion long ago, and knew he was doomed to a fall from great heights. This was about not taking down all those around him, and one person specifically, although

Alex had already come to the realization that it was far beyond his powers to do so. He had to return to Stawson. He had to return to the source, if only to absolve himself of an accumulation of past, present, and future wrongdoing. Alex wished that he could be more transparent with Marilina, but he knew in his unfeeling, armor-plated soul of souls that she would resign herself to pronouncement of a simple epitaph that might read like, "Whatever happened to Poor Alex followed him to the grave." Marilina understood full well that he would leave no trace, course, or shadow of what had truly ailed him, and that she might spend the rest of her days deciphering the hieroglyphics of his life; that is, if disposed to do so, for lack of a more rewarding earthly pastime for an idle mind.

Alex's guilt and utter disdain for himself, for what he continued to put Marilina through, became evident in his quotidian countenance. He was no different than a drug addict, alcoholic, or chain smoker, fully aware of the havoc wreaked on those around him, and, yet, absolutely powerless to stem the flow of those tides. Frankly, with senses dulled and energy sapped, he was dead in the water. The dynamo known as FOY1, while increasing the surge of his thoughts, emotions, and physical output, had done nothing to increase the efficiency of his bioenergy management. While he could not really fathom the drug's effects on his underlying physiology, he had certainly come to suspect and respect its end-result, over the years. Its imponent grip left him impotent to the onslaught of future shock. He was left no alternative but to chart the only remaining course available, in those sea lanes of the mind and soul that leave no room for status quo or instrument navigation. Had Stawson told him that only about one-third of the body's protein stores can normally be used for energy production to sustain mental and physical circuitry, and that FOY1 might even deplete those stores, he might never have embarked on this "suicide raid." With little or no noticeable increase lately in vital function owed to the drug, Alex was no more than a slave or indentured servant to the whims and machinations of a witch doctor and his nucleotide-driven, kitchen-cooked potion.

It was now or never. He had to let go of this, his current life. Alex still had many things to do and see, before expiration date precluded further forays into an unknown justified by predetermined calculated risk. A return to the "Mad Doctor" was imminent, but he did not know how to break the news to his soul mate. He would neither be bound by her tears after said revelation, nor be able to comfort her in her pain. Life would go on, and, while she might attribute his existence to a bad dream and even coin new idioms to describe the monster that he was, she would hopefully get over it; although there were no guarantees. For his part, regardless of his physical location, Alex would always be close to her; if not in his heart, then in the recesses of a cerebral attic cluttered with the refuse of what could have been. At the end of life's road, when paths would diverge, taking him to the Netherworld for his sins and her to a better place, there would be one last look, one last embrace, and one last ember on the fire of the spirit; before eternal separation and infinite "hard time" with no possibility of parole, for two lifetimes of misery wrought on souls, and one in particular, untarnished by the human condition until his appearance on the scene.

"I'm leaving," was Alex's good morning to a lover, who certainly deserved better.

"I know," was Marilina's inevitable reply, and the only one possible at that point, "but don't come back. From this moment on, you are dead to me."

As he pondered the body blow of those words, he was jolted to his senses by the clickety-clack and clatter of steel wheels on the rails leading from Stazione Termini to Aeroporto Fiumicino. Déjà vu. Steel wheels had also been his wake-up call on the rails leading from Marie Comanescu. Now, he was riding them once again. All his roads were leading away from Rome, and not back to Chicago just yet, but to San Francisco, where he would shed training wheels for wings to carry him to a showdown with the diabolical doctor.

11

Mended Wings

As the winged container glided between rolling hills into a landing pattern, set to deposit its damaged goods into a Bay Area holding pen, Alex could not help but ponder what he had left behind in Rome. He had certainly made the wrong decision, leaving Marilina and his new life behind; but the incessant urge to find himself, correct the uncorrectable, and find Stawson, in that order, had been simply too overpowering for him. He had all the time in the world. Stawson had seen to that, and, yet, there had to be some kind of expiration date sewn into the fabric of his genes. Alex knew that he might never see Marilina again, but the risk was well worth the price of his sanity.

His body was new, but his thoughts continued to return to the old. Alex continued to relive his childhood, at least in thought, in the overalls of an elder statesman. He remembered those Catholic catechism lessons of old, in which some lonely and buxom nun drilled platitudes and religious pomp and glory into his developing psyche. He had been more than fertile terrain for the pious pabulum of the day, and had even considered the priesthood in a moment of doubt, exaltation, and misdirection. Once, as a child of eight years, he had even convinced himself that he had, had a vision of the Almighty, during a round-trip, desert pilgrimage with his mother to Jerusalem. At that time, pure of heart and mind, he had sought only happiness and solace. Riches were as yet not an integral part of his mindset, and a life of service to his fellow man was a lesser of all evils, a road less traveled, and, yet, one that would fulfill the hopes and aspirations of a simple and unselfish lad.

While those times had long ago passed, similar reality checks that sometimes brought the false into perspective and helped jettison delusion were returning to him with a fury. Archangel and devil vied for his soul, as the image of his favorite childhood sex symbol in a habit, Sister Mary Rose, came to mind with her soft voice, gentle admonitions, and gestures studied to ward off evil eye, fire, and brimstone; as well as captivate young boys with a "take no prisoners" approach. Her words had, had a profound impact on Alex, as he came to the realization, short-lived as it was, that the happiest people don't have the best of everything; that they just make the best of everything they have. At that time, Alex became full of religious fervor and a determination that would have made even the indomitable General George Patton proud. Under the direction of Sister Mary Rose, he lived simply, loved generously, cared deeply, spoke kindly, learned Latin, and left the rest to God. In short, trust, kindness, honesty, and caring became the mantras of an eight-year-old boy; one who became convinced that the richest person was not the one who had the most, but the one who needed the least. Sure, Alex had been repressed and naïve at that tender, young age, but, as ignorance was, indeed, bliss, he was content to proceed through life with a toned-down vengeance and a soft-core mission. Damn the torpedoes of Farragut, he would win life's battles decisively, with a turn of the cheek.

How short-lived. What an effect a half century and insurmountable cold showers can have on an innocent mind. A man's mark on the world, after all, depending on which side of the fence he finds himself on, is not gauged by the goodness he embodies, but rather by the statement he makes. Adolph Hitler might certainly have attested to that.

Suddenly, Alex was jolted back to reality, as he descended the escalator to the baggage area, with subsequent embarkation on a new adventure, this time in the "City by the Bay." What he was looking for was not happiness, per se, but a justification for all the errors he had made in one lifetime, and was continuing to make in two. Perhaps it was not Stawson he should blame, but the Creator himself, as self-blame implied a full deck, and Alex was certainly not playing with one. All Stawson had done was choose the terrain, the playing field. He could not be held accountable for poor "grounds keeping," or could he? Why had the doctor chosen to use him in his as yet dubious experiment? How could he have been so unaware that Alex was neither a suitable subject for his work nor a shadow of the latter, but rather a shadow of a shadow? These and other cerebral calisthenics, as serious and necessary as they might be for his future existence, were nonetheless momentarily interrupted, as he reached the bottom of the escalator, by a bearded visage tantamount to how this was all going to end.

"Got some change?" was the inevitable query. Why was this no surprise to Alex?

"Here you go." A dollar fifty in change should have done the trick.

"That's it, man? That's all you can do? C'mon. I just got out of prison."

Alex was speechless. Even the homeless had become arrogant. If this homecoming was any indication of how life in San Francisco was going to proceed, then he had made a terrible mistake. Too late now. As he increased the distance between himself and the pauper, he turned to flip him some additional coin; more than ready to flip him something else were he not to be placated by the gesture. He thought he heard a curse of some kind, as he broke communication with the being, who most likely was a carrier of HIV and God only knew what else, and made a beeline for the baggage claim area. With mind one-track and bent on finding suitable living quarters in short order, Alex knew that his work was cut out for him. Once again, he would be starting over. Once again, he would be reconnoitering an old "stomping grounds," in which old friends and acquaintances most assuredly no longer existed, and in which he might find no further happiness than the fleeting kind already left behind in the Eternal City.

Where to go? What to do first? Thoughts raced through his head. A kaleidoscope of images sought to take the high ground of his mind. Alcatraz, Market Street, Golden Gate Park, Fisherman's Wharf, and the Castro area, all a part of the life he had led and then left eons ago. Would they be the same? Did it matter anyway? With all the time in the world on his hands and money in his pocket, anything and everything was fair game. First, however, he would have to establish a comfortable base of operations. On first and only thought, the Fairmont Hotel seemed the logical choice. The quotidian would follow, in due course, with Alex's choice for a permanent living arrangement being the Berkeley Hills. So, check in he did in a sumptuous suite at the Fairmont, ordering a room service diet consisting of a roasted chicken, brussel sprouts, and Swedish pastries, a far cry from the cuisine of emperors, gladiators, and the legions. There would be time enough on the morrow to scrutinize the terrain and put together a plan of attack.

Meal, shower, and low glow and hum of the television screen passed uneventfully. It was early evening, and, frankly, Alex did not have it in him to hit the streets. After all, the relative safety of Rome had ceded the day to a potpourri of vagabonds and street people, for which the Bay Area was famous and who would be all too ready to pounce upon a hapless tourist far away from home. Setting out on foot the next day would require all of Alex's innate skills of perception and foolhardiness, honed over years of biting off more than he could chew, eating crow, and being too dumb to know better. He was a showman, after all, the U.S. was his turf, and there would be no language barrier to contend with. Mingling with the natives would be tantamount to keeping the hands in one's pockets and jewelry out of sight, avoiding nocturnal "hot spots," like the City Hall area, which had become seedy at night, and speaking no more than necessary to a mixed Caucasian, Oriental, African American, Hispanic, and race of the day population that peacefully coexisted on the fringes of a dry powder keg, set to go off and up in flames at the least hint of earthquake, spark, or political or economic cataclysm. As he drifted off into a sleep more physically recuperative than mentally peaceful, his last thoughts and visions were of Marilina, and he was reminded of what he had left behind across two continents and an ocean. The morning light would bring adventure. He was sure of it. The night's gentle silence was filled with the jewels, Byzantine glass, church relics, Persian poetry, books of Cabala, atlases, and astronomical charts of a Sultan's mariner, about to embark on still another voyage of exploration; this time of a people and a seaside treasure trove built on a fault line.

As he rose with the birds, more akin to Rachel Carson's Silent Spring than a fertile flora and fauna watershed, nine hours later, Alex was smitten by a texture of sound far different from that of the Old World. The blaring of horns and mufflers created a cacophony that made the put-put concerto of Rome's Vespas and motorini sound like the gentle touch of Debussy on ivory. Off with the monogrammed bathrobe and into the steam of the shower, again, that turned the skin red. There was no turning back now for Alex. He was about to make, or repeat, history, for better or worse. As he patted dry the moisture, powdered, shaved, brushed, combed, perfumed, dressed, and otherwise donned the outward vestiges or armor for the day, he was overcome by an unexpected, and not unwelcome, air of confidence. One final look in the mirror told him that he still had it, whatever that "it" might be. There was neither wrinkle nor age line on his visage, which, if nothing else, indicated that Stawson's work in progress was well on the road to somewhere; final destination continuing to perplex, but for the immediate, relegated to the backburner of ongoing enigma.

"Will you be staying with us long, Mr. Bales?" was the desk clerk's incantation as Alex rounded the lobby desk on the catapult jolt toward the revolving doors of the Fairmont's main entrance.

"Long enough," was the terse reply, "about a week." Then he was through the circle of glass.

Forgoing four-wheeled steeds for the much slower rhythmic clip of shoes to pavement, Alex imbibed the brisk morning air with a hunger bordering on depression-era famine. He was at once both at peace and in a state of perpetual agitation. So many questions, so little time, and so much soul searching to do. With final destination on this trek immediately unknown and not wholly desirable for his boarding pass through life and the streets of San Francisco, he was coming as close to happiness at that particular moment as human physiology and the ghosts in his closet would permit. The sights and sounds of the streets were his allies, and, yet, the collection of languages he was perceiving went far beyond his limited linguistics intellect to decipher. No problem, he thought. While mere mortals might only have time to trade in the horseflesh of but a handful of great languages, Alex had been gifted by Stawson with innumerable linguistic lifetimes. It was all there for the taking, that is, as long as the FOY1 potion worked its magic, and who could be sure how long that would be.

Had the complexion of the U.S. and urban sprawl changed over the years, or was Alex now just more attuned to its ebb and flow? As he gazed about at the grins, grimaces, smiles, smirks, and scowls of those around him, he was reminded of a time ages ago in the same place when, as a summer exchange student at the University of California at Berkeley, he had been struck by similar countenances. Life had gone full circle, and, for better or worse, he was still here. There was, indeed, a lesson to be learned from all this. It was the age-old story of a return to youth. The latter, however, when not buttressed by hard, cold cash, was incapable of transporting the possessor of the fountain of youth to exotic places. Youth and money, with a good dose of the desire to learn, were all equally important. Alex ruminated on this. A life of study would allow one to earn the greenbacks required to explore the places others could only read about. A "normal" life, without the frills that financial independence brings, could permit one to only scan travel magazines, with neither the cultural or economic wherewithal to plant foot on terrains of heart's desire. And then there were the fringe benefits of the almighty dollar, as who hasn't employed the popular idiom and cultural sign o' the times, "No money, no honey."

For some unknown reason, and with an urgency not even he could comprehend, he was drawn to Chinatown. Granted, world travelers are frequently drawn mysteriously to the same places a second time, taking a leap of calculated risk, not faith, into well-trodden rabbit holes. Alex sought to recapture those days of old when, as a young collegiate, he would purchase a whole Pacific crab in one of the out-of-the-way, putrid and unhygienic, hole-in-the-wall fisheries, that went by the euphemistic appellation of "fish market," and populated the side streets, byways, and boweries of the "China on the Bay" underbelly. In those days, his fresh treasure would be pulled from a salted, water tank, placed between the crusted pages of a week-old newspaper whose yellowing edges were folded slightly at the borders, and ceded to him, to be tucked under arm, only when what was then a pittance was handed over to the illegal immigrant with missing front teeth who managed a counter under the watchful eye of some unseen shadow merging seamlessly with a dark corner of the establishment. Alex would then go about his business for the day, his "chelipeded" friend in hibernation and tow, until reaching his abode in the evening, and freeing his sleeping companion in the kitchen sink for a brief cleaning and resuscitation; before plunging him (or her) into a cauldron of boiling water and crab mix. Those were the days. While fast forwarding to the present would not permit a complete return to the future, it might perhaps provide Alex with a bit of that inner solace and peace, which he so desperately sought, and which might bring answers to questions obvious to others but cryptic to the self-possessed and ailing. His very worst impulses seemed to dissipate as soon as he crossed the threshold of the large Chinese arch that stood guard at the edge of Chinatown, and touched Chinese pavement again. He was reborn, at least for the time being. The planets were aligned as they should be, and an undertone of anticipated pleasure and excitement began to well up inside of him and stimulate neural circuits that had long ago been detoured. Caution and guarded anticipation, however, were his constant companions, at this point, as he had seen it all before, and the "Marilina debacle" was still fresh in his cluttered mind. He was also fully cognizant of the fact that the best of an individual effort can die at the end of a single generation or lifetime, and he was already working on two.

That aching, gnawing feeling in the stomach sounded the alarm bells of hunger, and Alex, more than obedient to his gastric juices, unceremoniously violated the inner sanctum of one of the hundreds of "Ma and Pa," Chinese eateries that populated his current turf. He was careful to scrutinize the clientele for tourists, as that would be an immediate signal to change locale. Only a "dive" with a local flavor, minus the English language, would do. It had served him in good stead in the past, and would most certainly do so again. Alex was becoming sated not by food for thought or stomach, but by a feeling of discovery. He had stumbled upon this place, with its fair share of dead cockroaches under the diner-type tables, by mere chance, and the faded and stained linoleum floor with its missing tiles, the odors, more akin to perfumes to him, of dead fish, entrails, and chowder, and the devil-may-care attitude of the Chinese expatriates chowing down on staples they had brought to the New World from port cities lost to them when they fled Red Chinese, Communist oppression and the poverty of the mother ship, convinced Alex that he was in the right place. Perhaps Stawson had done him a favor, after all. Allowing him a glimpse of the past, as fleeting as it might be, would perhaps be worth its weight in either gold or a continuum of unfettered depression. Alex had sought a place just like this, simply because he remembered it. Nothing was different, although it should have been, and this troubled him. He was alone, as in times gone by, feasting on morsels, the names of which he could not pronounce, and contemplating a next move in a chess game he knew he was losing, but refused to concede. Carpe diem, seize the day. Those words reverberated in his mind, if not his soul.

Now, Alex was fully aware that any food might turn on him. While he was not particularly fond of an "everything in moderation" approach, when it came to food, sex, drink, and inner demons, food poisoning was certainly not on his agenda. Even vitamins and fish oils, in high doses, could turn on a hapless victim or "health nut," making for interesting pro-oxidant, cancer-causing cocktails to riddle the body with invisible bullets mortally wounding genes, cells, and healthy, protective mutations. Charles Darwin had, had an inkling of this, Linus Carl Pauling had spent a lifetime trying to prove it, and Alex had no reason to be a disbeliever. Everything in the tea leaves pointed to his life of uncensored, unadulterated failure, based on excesses that he knew would ultimately take him down the unbeaten track to disaster. The strange thing was that he knew better, and, yet, up to now, had been powerless to unseal his fate. It was time for a change.

And, then, there she was. It was all happening again. Her face was well-chiseled, more akin to that of a Nordic Amazon than a feminine Greek goddess of delicate cloth. The turquoise of her eyes lit up the room, and her toned musculature was evidence of a good part of her twenty-eight or so years spent in the gym. She was a far cry, physically speaking, and a different kind of beauty from the olive-skinned Roman enchantress he had left an ocean away. With milky white skin and breasts supple and firm, not to mention ample, this was a walking-talking poster girl for a women's health club or collegiate varsity team. She, in fact, exuded fitness, and that was just what Alex needed in his current depressed, anemic, and lethargic state. Her white silk blouse and tight-fitting designer jeans, the way she moved her lips as she jawed the rubbery texture of her fish stew, and the hint of a smile on her face, as her eyes met his in a momentary stare that lasted a second longer than he had intended and gave him away, all promised nights of unparalleled passion, if only he might drop a word to her. Seated alone at a nearby table and in an obvious rapture fed by the culinary delight that lay before her, she looked every bit the part of the professional graduate student by day and sex symbol after dark. Yes, whether she was a rigid academic or student of the world, she was most definitely a handsome specimen and beautiful woman. There was no denying it. On the other hand, and there is always another hand, on this turf and in this neck of the woods, she might be a byproduct of the lesbian culture that she quite obviously embodied, at least in Alex's mind. There was only one way to find out. It wouldn't be easy. Goaded by his chagrin at his own shyness, especially in a second lifetime that should have quite honestly armed him with powers of self-confidence and egotism far beyond those of mortal men, he decided to act.

As he asked for the check and waited the obligatory ten minutes to be accommodated, before making a beeline for the cash register on the Formica countertop that was standard fare in an operation of this kind, he scribbled his first and last name, room number, Fairmont Hotel, and its telephone number on a paper napkin of inferior quality, that nonetheless stood up to the rigors of his ballpoint pen. This was do or die, with only a slight margin of error acceptable. Then, again, what did Alex have to lose? He had been placed in this position so many times before, that one more caused hardly a ruffle in his armament of chicken feathers. As he rose, check and folded paper napkin in the left of his two hands, he glided effortlessly past the table of the center of his attention, dropping the napkin within inches of her outstretched left hand, while continuing to proceed to the payment counter. He paid for his meal in cash, as the time to process plastic would have left him for far too long in a position of vulnerability and hard questions from the rear. He never looked back, as he negotiated the tiny front exit of the "slumeatery" (slum eatery), as he would have coined it, and made a left for an instinctive pavement introitus leading to trolley cars, Bay Area Rapid Transit (BART), Fisherman's Wharf, Golden Gate Park, Alcatraz, or any number of other possible destinations, with no definite direction or route in mind. Contemplating an old Alpha Sigma Phi Fraternity saying from his first lifetime, that, "The cause is hidden, the results well known" (Causa Latet Vis Est Notissima), Alex became acutely aware that he was treading, and with some trepidation, those same waters that had lapped his fraternity initiation. With no set course in his second life, no final destination charted, no object of love at that moment except for a romantic advance on woman who hardly knew he existed until the awkward display of a worn-out napkin, and no goals but a brash death wish if "things," heretofore completely unspecified, did not go his way, he was floundering in much the same way as a fraternity pledge on "hell weekend;" with no support network, friend in the world, or means of transport back to lucidity from real dream.

Then it hit him like a brick wall. As Alex turned to the right to face the pedestrians on the opposite side of one of Chinatown's exit byways, he was struck by a vision no less cold and heartless than Medusa's glare. There, staring at him, not more than fifty feet away, as the crow flies and on the sidewalk corner, were Edward Stawson, Marie Comanescu, Jill, and the homeless gentleman from the air terminal, or "succubus" as Alex in a split second preferred to refer to him; all with eyes fixed on his immediate position. Closing and opening his eyes, to erase what he thought was an imaginary vision, did not cancel the imprint on his retina. A second blink and contraction of his bilateral eye-closure muscles, and they were gone. Had he imagined all this, or was something far more sinister at play? Trembling brought neither frictional warmth nor the physiological "fight or flight" response. He was dead in the water, for all practical purposes, and inertia bred further fear. It would pass. Alex at least hoped it would. Sometimes the best laid plans, however, fail to come to fruition. He could not be certain of what he had seen. In the fragile condition of his mind, if not his body, hallucinations, delusions, and illusions were as commonplace as fast-food skylines. If his vision were real, on the other hand, then he was neither a free spirit nor free of the Stawson nightmare. A single notion became ever clearer to him, crystal clear. We are all slaves to our lives, be they first or second passages, and to those around us. There is no real freedom. We curse, we declare our independence, and we howl at the moon, only to be swamped by the everyday, the mundane, and the ties that bind. Let a man tell you he's free, and there you have a man with balls too small to admit the complete opposite.

The vision of his nemesis and company, while troubling, to say the least, was not enough to completely blemish his day or truncate his jaunt. He made for the nearest BART station, and hopped on the line that would take him under the San Francisco Bay to Oakland, with final destination Berkeley. With no one to love, not even himself, little to hope for, and absolutely nothing to do, he felt vagabondage in a quest to satisfy his wanderlust might be a good way to spend the rest of the day. His trip to Berkeley with its multivariate coffee houses, numerous independent record shops, small vegetarian hide-away restaurants, and New Age, storefront spas was a no better nor worse urban endpoint than any other in his otherwise dreary existence. What the heck. He might even find a decent, long-term living condition in the Berkeley Hills.

Anything and everything was fair game. So, after a brief, three p.m., decaffeinated plunge in a coffee house across the street from the UC-Berkeley campus, Alex boarded a crowded bus for the ascent to the Berkeley Hills and the rustic homes hidden away there and camouflaged by a variegate fauna and flora. His immediate goal would be to rent a home, but which? He knew no one in the immediate area, and the last time he had made this foray was forty years ago. While his memory for detail was up to ship, it was more attuned to subject matter like where one might find the best frozen yogurt on Telegraph Avenue or in downtown Berkeley, not the layout or geography of residential areas. Ask him where the best "pick-up" joint in the Bay Area was, and he would have told you the downtown Safeway grocery store, without batting an eye. Ask him, on the other hand, where to find a suitable residence in Berkeley, and he'd clamp up before your very eyes, as doubts set in.

As he walked the tree-covered streets with a view of San Francisco across the bay, Alex was struck by the fact that he couldn't retrace his steps in those narrow paths he traversed, even if he had wanted to. For all practical purposes, he was lost. So, the only thing to do was trudge onward. Sooner or later, he would stumble upon a "For Rent" sign on a leaf-covered lawn or in a front room window. It was only a question of time and the relative hardiness of his fallen arches. He had not read the Want Ads or rental section of the *San Francisco Chronicle*, the *San Francisco Examiner*, the *Berkeley Daily Planet*, the *Berkeley Voice*, or the *Daily Californian*, so he was basically running blind. Better to be uninformed and the latter, than misinformed by the press, he rationalized, although not completely convinced. He turned a corner into an alleyway, and proceeded down its causeway, behind the neat rows of sparse housing and lined by oversized trash bins filled to the brim with bush and tree trimmings, the food of mulch. Reaching the halfway point, Alex was about to turn back, when he spotted it. Clear as day, or dusk, at this point, in the window of a backyard shed or garage converted into a bungalow was the hand printed sign he had sought. "Small room for rent," it said. "Kitchen and bath. Inquire inside."

That was all it took to get the blood flowing through the femorals to his legs; and moments later, after what turned out to be a mad dash for the adjoining home's front door, he put index finger to the doorbell, spit on his hands to brush back his hair, and mouthed a smile as wild and untamed as the natural surroundings of this wooded environment. While not jocular by nature, and prone to poor interviewing skills, unsurely outward visage, and rebellious body language, Alex would make every effort to pass this "audition." Mending his wings would depend on it. The door opened, and his fate was sealed. Or was it?

12

Blow Out

Frozen in his tracks was an understatement. Just what were the chances of lightning striking in the same place twice, someone winning the multimillion-dollar state lottery more than once, or hitting a hole-in-one on the golf course? And, yet, it had happened. While not himself hunting or seeking retribution from monsters, it now appeared that they were hunting him. Alex, for all his sins and imperfections, didn't deserve the lot that had been cast in his favor. He had drawn the short straw, and, consequently, at least in his own mind, he was not getting a fair shake. The words of an old college chum, more entrepreneur and self-made Renaissance man than student, came to mind at that moment. "You don't get what you deserve in life; you get what you can negotiate." What a revelation, forty years later. Life was coming full circle, as there she stood in the doorway. It was impossible, but there she was. How totally sinister, Stawson & Company had been. There was no proof of the witchdoctor's involvement, and no choice but to forge ahead. Maybe he should kill himself. He had certainly thought about it on more than five occasions, but resignation and endgame were inversely proportional to what FOY1 had represented to Alex. Life was much too glorious to end to the sound of a pistol shot. It was high time for the cursed, the damned, and the utterly lost, like Alex, to stand up and be counted, although not in negative numbers. Mettle could be demonstrated in any number of ways, all of which escaped him at that moment. Whether Stawson be doctor, demon, or something far worse was of little or no consequence. It had to end, and end soon.

Her stare embodied an enigma; her appearance, an answer to his prayers. It would end soon, whether by silver bullet, crucifix, or purifying fire. Words had to be uttered, and uttered quickly, as he stood before the golden-locked Amazon he had crossed paths with hours before in the Chinese seafood "slop shop." Words would be awkward, but must now become standard equipment.

"Haven't we met before?" was the best Alex could do.

"Not exactly, unless you count sleight of hand and slip of napkin," was the immediate retort from the now smiling vixen.

Where was he going to go with this? Embarrassment held full sway, as he formulated a rear action to culminate in counterattack. The entire exchange of friendly hostilities would hinge on his next line. Alex knew this, and, yet, cold-turkey cleverness and improvisation were not his fortes, at least not in this lifetime.

"I need a place to live."

"I beg your pardon?"

"I need a place to live. I am lost, and trying to find myself. If I told you anything else, you wouldn't believe me. I had no idea you lived here, and I certainly did not follow you home. Please, make no mistake about it, I need your help."

That was much too much information. What had possessed him? This woman was a complete stranger. He hadn't even gotten her name, but that didn't stop him from spilling his guts. Dumb ass! How could he be so stupid? He braced himself for the inevitable door slam in his face.

It wasn't forthcoming, however, just a "C'mon in."

As he crossed the threshold of the two-story bungalow set deep in the wooded Berkeley hills, a castle in the Carpathian Mountains was not lost on him. Was he the spider, the fly, or just an innocent bystander? Had he fixated irrevocably on the keeper of the keep, and her impression of his projected image, instead of arming himself to the hilt against a stake to the heart of his vulnerability? A cursory inspection of the home's ample foyer revealed no religious amulets, artifacts, or symbols. Good sign or bad, Alex knew not. He would see this thing through, however, as he followed the object of his

curiosity and desire to a comfortable living room area, complete with crack-
ling, spitting conflagration in its rustic fireplace. The fires of hell, he thought,
or, perhaps, with only a slight stretch of the imagination, the fires of ardor
burning within him.

"Have a seat." She motioned for him to nestle on a comfortable or-
ange-leather sofa, which gave off the distinct, yet not unpleasant, smell of
Copenhagen Furniture dollar signs. The room was tasteful at a glance, the
woman no slouch, and the outward signs, symptoms, vestiges, and aromas
of old money neither irritating to the eye nor bitter to the palate, respectively.
All things being equal, a rich woman vastly outpaced and outclassed a lowly
counterpart or the honest, humble, and modest homemaker that mothers
deferred to, for the "apples of their eyes." The initial attempts at conversation
would not come easy. They never did. Then, again, this entire change of events
was just too strange to have been left up to mere chance. There were forces at
play here that went far beyond his mortal reach, and Alex was simply along for
the ride. Like the gambler that he was, he would toss in his chips and call. He
wanted to see the hand of the companion in crime, adversary, or netherworld
being who now sat directly opposite him.

"Thank you," he heard himself intone, to the offer to perch on the sofa.

"My name is Kalli Hallings, and it looks like you could use a friend. Now,
don't mistake my kindness for a green light. Our encounter at the restaurant
this afternoon, I must admit, was a bit, shall we say, esoteric or even cryptic."

"I would say fortuitous, if I may interrupt, at least on my end. Let me be
perfectly frank. You don't know me, and you certainly don't owe me anything.
I've been out of the country for quite some time, trying to find myself, and now
I'm back. The simplest things, like finding a room, have become extremely
complicated for me. I need your help."

The look on Kalli's inquisitive, if not unsettled, face said it all. "Where
are you headed?" That said it all, too.

"It depends on whether you mean in this world or the next," was Alex's
immediate reply. The verbal exchange had taken a turn for the worse. It was
not going the way he wanted it to. There was no going back now, diluting his
existential scent, or camouflaging his soul's skin to Kalli's slow, deliberate,
and relentless pursuit of the truth. She would think he was a kook, or, at the
least, a closet nut case. Turning around and high-tailing it out of there was not
an option, however. He needed to proceed, cost whatever it might cost. What
did he have to lose? They were only living quarters. Failure would not be the

end of the world, just a detour to San Francisco International Airport to board a silver bird for a return trip to Chicago; in order to keep an appointment with a dresser drawer and the coroner, or to mosey on down to the suburbs for a showdown with the powers that be, aka Edward Stawson, by whatever name he now went by, or whatever form he now took.

"What do you mean?"

"If you're referring to present time and place," Alex interjected, "the Bay Area is as good a place as any for me to plant some albeit temporary roots. If the long-term is your query, then hell is my answer, the same place all people like me end up."

Kalli, not missing a beat, focused on her prey. "Maybe you should go live in town."

"I've been to town," came his knee-jerk response. "It's a good thing my inner demons come in multiples of one. Otherwise, I'd have five to match every place I've lived in my lives."

"Lives, you say?"

"I meant life." That slip-up could have been costly. He went on, "They say the Rocky Mountains are the marrow of the world. If that be the case, then New York, San Francisco, Chicago, and Rome are the pulse, lungs, liver, and spirit, respectively. I've lived in them all, for one period of time or another, and I can say with all honesty that the four of them alone have both stimulated and thoroughly exhausted me more than any other fifty put together."

"I've always felt," Kalli began, "that with a fair wind at your back and eyes to the sky, one can live anywhere. Now, it's getting dark outside, and times a wastin'. While my gut tells me you are damaged goods, I can't help but feel there's something inherently positive about you. Make no bones about it, I want to rent my backyard apartment. If that means, however, surrounding myself with negative energy, then it can remain vacant till kingdom come. I'll show it to you. If you like it, it's nine hundred dollars a month, utilities included. Take it, or leave it."

Sight unseen, there was no doubt in his mind, but that he would take the apartment bungalow. A superficial tour of the place would be totally un-necessary, but he would go along with it anyway, with little coaxing from his hostess-to-be-landlord. Actually, it was quite cozy, bordering on an enlarged backyard shed with all the comforts of home, including kitchen area with large table, small bathroom with shower, and a single room doubling as a living room and bedroom. The latter housed a beige, cloth sofa that had seen better days, from which a foldout bed could be regurgitated on demand. Both bed and sofa were comfortable, and smelled of neither animal nor yesterday's leftovers. The large picture windows on three sides of the shed, apartment, or bungalow, whichever term, owner, tenant, or point of view dictated, while providing little security and substantial loss of privacy, were eyes to nature and an outside world that bore the promise of rugged adventure and a breath of fresh air long choked out of congested city streets.

Alex would be completely content with his new abode, like it or not, although his goal, i.e., the big picture, was to eventually relocate to the Amazon's "fortifications;" namely, Kalli's not all together humble, but extremely tasteful and well-appointed domain. That would be his quest and Holy Grail, at least for the immediate future. There was no guilt in his heart for harboring such an agenda. After all, he was a man, first and foremost, and his only sin was to have sold his soul to the devil, or whatever or whomever Stawson purported to be. Alex represented the best and worst of the human race, sucking the marrow and life's blood out of the very earth that should otherwise have been equal opportunity and even-handed with all, in order to live another day on the road to another lifetime.

It is said that the ability to compromise makes a man noble. If that be the case, then Alex was as ignoble a creature as man, monster, or God had ever produced, for he wanted it all. There was no telling how far he would go to reach that end, either. Aspiration attainment, in Alex's mind, implied not wiping everyone out. Just his enemies, that's all. If need be, himself, too.

And, so, the days passed, uneventfully for those with but one life to live; frenzied and manic with excitement for him who had injected wrinkles, aging, and the cycles of life away. For him, circadian rhythms held no more influence than sunlight on hidden stalactites and stalagmites. His life began to revolve around just one thing, and her name was Kalli. The following four months, between August and November, were among the happiest he could recall. Alex remembered each and every day, each and every moment, as if they were tattooed to the retina of his mind's eye. What started out slowly as a tumbling snowdrift suddenly took on the proportions of a raging avalanche. Kalli, at first so timid that she could not even invite him over for dinner without breaking into a facial flush, became both predator and prey in a little over two weeks.

They became inseparable friends, allies, and lovers, if not in that order, and spent sleepless nights in each other's arms and wakeful daily jaunts on the town, dividing their attention between Turkish baths and health spas, farmers' markets, coffee houses, artsy movie venues, Japanese restaurants, and the vegan in-crowd. Alex learned to "loosen his anus," live a bit, and dabble in Buddhism, the Unitarian Church, goddess worship, séances, astrology, star adoration, and Zen. Frankly, he liked what he was doing, and what that was, was basically doing nothing. Living life the second time around, so to speak, was much more hedonistic, if not all together fulfilling, than a single shot. Epicurus would have been proud of him. Alex was doing everything he wanted, when he wanted, and with whom he wanted. Who could have asked for more? A television commercial came to mind, "If you like what you do for a living, you never work a day in your life." He might have changed it ever so cosmetically to, "If you like what you do in your second living, then you needn't dwell or harp on your first." Perhaps Stawson hadn't been so bad, after all.

Alex would often daydream about his good fortune, and reminisce on how his idyllic interlude with Kalli had taken shape. Those very first two weeks in the bungalow had been traumatic, not because of his new surroundings, per se, but owed exclusively to the wood, mortar, brick, cement, and self-doubt that had physically and existentially separated Alex from the object of his desire. Two weeks, fourteen days, twenty thousand, one hundred and sixty minutes, or any other way it was looked at, had been a more than sufficient wakeup call to action. He would lie, cheat, steal, and/or deceive to get into her pants, or panties, and then her mind, if not vice versa. He was more than certain that his ultimate happiness lay there, and he would arrive by hook or crook. Pretense would be on his side. While the angel on his right shoulder might say, "When you act like that, you're no better than the vilest of the species," the devil on his left shoulder would win the day with the exhortation that, "When you're in the mud with the pigs, you don't don a tuxedo and clean the dirt under your fingernails." Alex had even coined a short stanza or verse, while seated on his favorite thinking bin, otherwise known as the toilet, to describe how he would conquer the heart and mind of the Amazon. It went something like this:

Go with the flow,
Lie through your teeth,
Treat direct question,
Like looter or thief.

Proud he was not for what he had become or to what extremes he would go to attain his grail, booty, or "booty call," but, then, again, there would be no turning back now. The die was cast. He would see this thing through to the end, and he did, at least in this installment of his second lifetime. It started out with dinners, six to be exact, and all in Kalli's home, during the first two-week lead-up to idyllic bliss. Alex did not know how to react, let alone act. This woman both excited and scared him to death, and he, with two lifetimes'-worth of experience. She was a doctoral candidate in philosophy at UC-Berkeley, and she maintained a fervid interest in Oriental religions and astrology. Perhaps a bit off the wall she was, but that only added to her allure. Those two weeks passed in the bat of an eye, and the two potential lovebirds did not sleep together, although the topic was broached on more than one occasion. It was decided that the momentous event would take place at their next encounter, although it never did. That would have extinguished the flicker of spontaneity before it ever burned brightly between them. Nevertheless, Alex was getting anxious and frustrated. He wanted desperately to touch her, and feel every nook and cranny of her body, before he further dissected her mind. Both the physical and the mental held so much promise, and he envisioned the glorious years ahead at his disposal to explore the one and the other. One uneventful evening together he could contain himself no longer.

"You know, you promised," he began.

She knew immediately where this was going. "I know, but it's just not right yet. We hardly know each other."

"You promised." Alex sounded irritated. She was hardly a prude.

"Hmm," was Kalli's onomatopoetic incantation. "Okay, let's go upstairs."

It was all so mechanical. Alex more or less begging for her sexual favors, and Kalli acceding to his desires only because she was a woman of her word. This was not the way it was supposed to be. This was not the way he had imagined it would be. This was not the way it actually did go down, or the way she actually did "go down." While Alex undressed in a fury to reveal his "Emperor's new clothes," brushed his teeth and gargled, as if the brilliance of the enamel and his sweet breath in some way correlated with his life that depended on them, and assumed the prone position and his sexiest pose on the down comforter that lay across the large double bed, which bordered on king-size, for the queen of the castle. He was made to wait an interminable length of time before his quarry appeared in black strapless bra and a miniscule thong at the doorway to the master bathroom. He became extremely aroused at the sight of Kalli's undergarments, which left little to the imagination, exposing her ample breasts and a love triangle fit more for the Kama Sutra than Pythagorean theorem. In any case, he would gauge the hidden dimensions of both.

That night, after all the awkwardness was said and done, they made love three times, collapsing into each other's arms after the "trifecta." Peaceful sleep came upon them both, so deep as to blunt all perception of glimmering candles, spilled plastic bottles of aromatic oils, continuous CD loops of Joni Mitchell and a veritable parade of romantic female recording artists, and stained, crumpled blankets, silk sheets, and goose down pillows dangling from bed corners and bedposts; all silent testimonies to the ravages of love and war. As sunlight picked its way through the Venetian blinds, gently nudging Alex back to consciousness, he realized he had fallen asleep inside her. How romantic, how exhilarating, and how thoroughly exhausting the festivities of the night before must have been. He would extricate himself from the precarious, yet blissful, chasm into which he had fallen, and position himself facing her, awaiting the signs of life, facial expressions, and body language posturing indicating "pass-fail."

It didn't take long before the new day's light, coupled with the as yet indecipherable power of a stare, his stare, on her unconscious mind, brought animation to her state of tranquil dormancy. Words would be awkward, and perhaps totally uncalled for, at this point. They always were. Nonetheless, one had to begin again somewhere.

"Sleep okay?" was Alex's weak attempt at verbosity.

"Fine, and you?"

"Can't complain. Oh, crap. I won't lie. That was the best night's sleep I've had in months. I know we hardly know each other, but I feel a comfort, a kind of safety and protection I can't explain, being here with you now," said the fly to the spider.

"I do, too," was Kalli's beaming response. "Let's cut the chit-chat. What do you want to do today? Your wish is my command, within limits, of course," was her playful thrust, awaiting his parry.

"We could stay in bed all day."

Although spoken with a glint in his eye, Alex's attempt at humor, or perhaps it was earnestness and downright sincerity, did not evoke the desired facial expression, words, or body language in Kalli. While hoping for a touch or some other sign of affection, affirmation, or accession to his whims or fancies, with the latter otherwise known as hungers or longings, he was met with undazzling blue eyes and a moment of surreal strangeness, before her inevitable matter-of-fact response.

"Oh, let's go out today. It's always so boring in the house."

So, that was that. Perhaps he hadn't been that great in bed. Perhaps Kalli was a strange fish, a closet lesbian, or had another agenda. Perhaps he was merely jumping to conclusions and making a hasty generalization, and should take her words at their face value. All these and other suppositions swelled the cramped confines of his cranium, and he sought answers to age-old questions that would not be immediately forthcoming. He would play along. To do anything else would be contrary to superego or conscious game plan.

"What's your desire, Mademoiselle?"

"Have you ever been to Alcatraz? That mischievous look in her eye had finally returned. Thank God, Alex reflected, or those spirits that move and shake the world, leaving us breathless and gasping for breath, at times hopeful, but for the most part thoroughly befuddled in the wake of their actions. Kalli continued, "It's a national park, I'm sure you know, that was once a federal prison, and it's only about a mile and a quarter from Fisherman's Wharf."

"Actually, it was a military fort back in eighteen fifty-four, that only became a federal prison later in nineteen thirty-four." Where did that come from? The perplexed look on Kalli's face said it all. This spouting of insignificant and inconsequential trivia or fun facts, on Alex's part, was totally unexpected, slightly refreshing, and a reminder to Kalli to not underestimate the force of nature or UMO ("Unidentified Manly Object") that had been laid on her doorstep. Alex quickly followed up with, "Don't ask me where I picked up that bit of useless information. Maybe it was on the back of a cereal box or deep in the bowels of the National Enquirer," he smirked.

"So, is it a go?"

"I'm completely in your hands, Kalli."

"I meant Alcatraz," was her playful retort.

"Affirmative. Let's go."

This was the first of many such glorious local road trips, which always ended in a night of passionate and heated lovemaking. What more could a mere mortal, or, rather, immortal, have asked for, whether it had been in a first, second, or any other lifetime? Alex, however, was more than just a little apprehensive in thinking that everything was proceeding, and continued to proceed, so nicely. There was nary a glitch in the chain of months that followed, and Murphy's law carried little or no weight in the arena dominated by the two love gladiators. It was too good to be true, and when it is, it is. Yet this was going to last. It had to. Longevity, with a capital "L," was the name of the game, and Alex swore a solemn oath to himself, although pledges were not something he inherently stuck to, that he would make it work; and that his relationship with Kalli would be a perpetual shining light in an otherwise dismal field of failures and string of defeats.

Then it happened. It always does. The gut punch to end all others came out of nowhere, and left him prostrate and gasping for breath. One morning, no different from the two hundred or so that had recently preceded it, Alex ejected from his bungalow after the usual large mug of gourmet "Joe," and made the short walk to Kalli's back door. By now, he and his Amazon bedded down together only on Friday and Saturday nights, and this was the beginning of a new week. He found Kalli's abode barred to entrance, at least from the rear. Strange. That had never occurred before. As his emergency protocol would have it, Alex would make a beeline for the long arc around the house, through the side gate, and out onto the front lawn, for pursuance of an amicable, conjugal "break-in" via the front door.

Something, however, was amiss. An unexpected sight, which no mortal or immortal eyes should see, greeted his advance around the corner of the residence. They had their backs to him. The vision of them stopped him in his tracks. Thank God they had not, as yet, zeroed in on him, zeroing in on them. There was still time to act. A cooler wit would dictate contingency plans to the wholesale horror, shock, and incredibility of the scene unfolding before his blinking and not all together accommodating eyes. As he backed around the corner again into the shadows, he couldn't shake the image of Kalli, Stawson, and his other henchmen, Marie, Jill, and the airport mendicant, all conversing like old chums, or like a hunting party honing strategies and readying weaponry for pursuit and eventual termination of their prey. How could this be happening? "My soul, that devil Stawson shall never have." Those were Alex's final words and war cry whisper, as he collapsed, unconscious, to a rustle of autumn leaves.

When he came to, a matter of seconds seeming like endless minutes later, his mind was besieged by a series of verses that had coalesced into a poem, during the darker days of his young adult life, when prospects had been slim and suicide loomed pervasively on the horizon. In those days, a lifetime ago, Alex had been riddled with troubles. Anger and sadness had been his calling cards, and he had often dwelled on the unpredictability of the human condition. How could a stork's joyous arrival, his, in fact, have later morphed into something so monstrous? Somewhere along the line, and in one way or another, he had become Mephistophelean, the title of his poem, and was absolutely defenseless to the onslaught. Could bad ever have become good, however? Stawson and his crown jewel, FOY1, were to have been his exorcism. Instead, they had become the gatekeepers to the dock of embarkation for his short but sweet ferryman's ride to the other side. While Charon was the fruit of a fertile imagination, Kalli was the product of the here and now, all too willing, in Alex's mind, to set a course in his company and skim waters flowing to the rhythms of Hades' bidding. The tides of salvation were quickly going out, as the window for a return trip narrowed precipitously, to the tune of incredulous betrayal. How could she have been party to such malevolence?

The words of the verses came back to him, in the form of an incantation, as Alex, in a flash of hindsight, contemplated the inevitability of his own failure and fall from grace in not one, but two lifetimes.

To do it again,
I would sell my soul,
To become life of the party,
Or play some kind of role.

Too many failures,
Birds in the hand,
Fires of hell,
Create glass from dry sand.

I gave it my all,
It tested my steel,
Kind words from a demon,
Rekindle lost zeal.

152

Say what you will,
Condemn me forever,
You ascend to the stars,
At my fall on the lever.

Pretty things,
Joyous laughter,
I want them all,
Damn sulfur's hereafter.

Perhaps it's too late,
My life's gone by,
And even the devil,
Can do nothing but sigh.

Nowhere to go,
To live out my years,
While others find peace,
I rejoice in my fears.

White dove in flight,
Hawk at the ready,
Ruin a good day,
Blood loss is steady.

Full speed ahead,
Down for the count,
Brimstone, a throne,
His right knee I mount.

Mephistophelean, I am,
I learned from no master,
Molds cast in Hades,
Are now filled with my plaster.

The momentary explosion of light from a dangling bauble cut short poetic license and temporarily halted a mind's downward spiral, as Alex looked up to see the hardened features of an incensed Amazon, bent on revenge for having been caught in an unnatural, if not wholly unholy, act. His bearing testimony had, in fact, condemned himself. The blowout was now complete.

13

The Best Defense

It was over. If looks could kill, reciprocal vaporization would have left no traces. All that remained was the formalities or the insults, whichever came first and dominant. No amount of explaining could possibly erase the vision that Alex had beheld, or dispel the rash of innuendo and hasty generalization that flooded the watershed of his inner sanctum. There would be no apologies, no petitions for clarification, and absolutely no remorse. Alex knew what he had to do, and time was of the essence, not to be wasted on a Stawson succubus. The "how" of how this happened was purposeless. The intricacy of the entire plot was beyond his very comprehension. There was only one thing left to do, and that was go back to the source. Kalli, per se, was inconsequential, and had been but a stringed implement in the hands of a master puppeteer. Whatever her price had been, it paled in comparison to the toll that had been exacted by FOY1 and its originator on Alex's mind, body, and being.

The glare in her eyes, momentarily held in check by a feeble attempt at subterfuge and dissuasion, was what Alex expected and what came.

"I guess you're surprised." It had begun.

"Understatement. I'll just get my things."

"Don't you want to know why?"

"No. The cookie jar just fell off the shelf."

Alex was now playing the role of the proverbial noble gentleman who says one thing, and thinks another. While dying to establish the "why" of the connection between Dr. Frankenstein and his once and not future paramour, he would not give Kalli that satisfaction. She was a small fish in the big picture, after all, and his best defense was a formidable and tactical retreat, to live and fight another day.

An abrupt turn and a beeline for his things in the bungalow were his final good-byes to a woman who had promised much at first encounter, only to deliver a deathblow to his ego and emotions at final parting. As he entered his premises, he sensed immediately that something was just not right. What could it be? He had been no stranger to surprises, of late. So, as he wheeled around and braced for the frigid impact of sudden recognition, he expected fewer mental flurries, cold shivers, and rattling bones than his most recent post-Stawson days had brought. There, on the couch that adorned his spartan living quarters, a dark shadow and a lit match proclaimed the triumphant return on the scene of Detective Joe Marbry. As Alex shrugged off intrusive and totally irrelevant thoughts of the important roles couches had played in the last six or seven years of his life, an inner voice invoked repeatedly, "Remember, you are only a man," as if to pay homage to Marilina and her Roman ancestors; followed by, "and so is he," as if to take the supernatural out of perspective and off the table in this rerun with Marbry.

"Going somewhere?" was the first verbal sword thrust coming from the ebony-colored Chicago praetorian, as he simultaneously flicked "on" both the lights of the small studio apartment and the safety of the 9mm "security blanket" he held in his right hand.

"What are you doing here, Marbry? It's been a long time," was Alex's gut response, instead of the more culpable, "How did you find me?"

His relentless pursuit of a lead, any lead, in the Randy Danhurst case had put Joe Marbry on the fine line between duty to the force and obsession. Something had just not added up. His twenty years as a detective in the Chicago Police Department had taught him that what flies below the radar screen is the invisible blip that holds the key to unsolved murders, serial slaughters, apparent homicides, unresolved kidnappings, and staged suicides. While he could not always put his finger on the guilty party or parties, if his opinion carried any weight whatsoever, he would always be there as judge, jury, executioner, and savior of the taxpayer dollar. The Danhurst case, six and a half years in and going nowhere, was not only a thorn in his side, but a nail driven into his very soul and still another reason why he had chosen law enforcement as a career in the first place.

"I won't beat around the bush, Mr. Bales," his violent youth and ghetto brogue precluded poetic parlance and sparring with four-syllable words. "I have never been convinced of your innocence. I can feel your guilt in my bones. You had something to do with Mr. Danhurst's death, and I'm going to bring you down. What did you think, that when I let you walk past me that morning in his apartment, that you were walking out of my life? You're as guilty as a mare on fertility injections, who has just brought to light a five-legged colt."

That last statement, indeed, triggered a chill down Alex's spine. Was Marbry in some way referring to the Stawson experiment? How could he possibly know about the "witch doctor?" And even if he did, what did that have to do with his friend Randy Danhurst's demise?

"Marbry, I don't know how you found me after all these years, and, frankly, I don't care. You have no jurisdiction here. So, go back to the Windy City, and let dead dogs lie. If you had hard evidence, there'd be more of you than just one, and you would have already cuffed me. Fuck off!"

"The story gets more interesting, Mr. Bales. When a dubious autopsy on your so-called friend, a less-than-respectable reputation turned up on your background check, a series of strange and unexplained clues in the Danhurst apartment, and a telephone call from a woman with an uncommon accent all followed suit, I decided to make you the star of my show; and I had you tailed. You were fooling no one with your movements, and your short trips to Oak Park, while carefully choreographed, were nonetheless easily shadowed by me, your invisible dance partner. I was one step behind you all the way, and sometimes a step ahead."

"Okay, Marbry, that's fine. What you have, however, is a big goose egg. What you have wouldn't even hold up in Judge Judy's courtroom, let alone the big leagues. So, again, with all due respect for your twenty years on the Chicago Police Force, locking up the good as well as the bad, it seems to me, fuck off!"

"Don't you want to hear more, Mr. Bales? There is more. I think you owe me that." Marbry could see the impatience in Alex's demeanor, and hoped he would not have to shoot for the legs, to prevent his bolt through the door.

"I owe you nothing, Marbry."

Without batting a lash or missing his cue, Marbry went on, "Two years into the Danhurst case, and with you having slipped through my fingers, it became evident to me that this entire affair was slowly but surely reaching the threshold for yet another 'cold case.' God knows I'd seen a few in my time."

"Leave God out of it, Marbry. This is your witch hunt."

"I became frustrated with myself, and began to doubt my own intuitive and deductive skills, all the while unable to let go of my conviction that you were as guilty as sin. With no hard evidence, however, and only a hunch to corroborate what you and I knew to be true, I started drinking a bit. Well, to make a long story short, booze, broads, and a nervous breakdown didn't make for a happy household. I came home one night to find my wife and two beautiful daughters gone for good."

"Don't expect me to shed a tear, Marbry."

"I haven't finished yet. I think you'll find the rest of my story interesting. If you don't, it is I who will hand you the gun. You can then put us both out of our misery."

"Go on. I've got a plane to catch. You have two minutes."

"With my life a mess and going nowhere, and my career in jeopardy, I felt the only way to sober up and salvage any good years left to me was to bring the Danhurst case to a successful conclusion. With no leads, however, I continued to drown my sorrows in a bottle."

"You'd better hurry up, Marbry, I'm getting ready to leave."

"Then," he continued, as if oblivious to Alex's impatience, "it came to me. I would go to the source. I was already under investigation by Internal Affairs for not only beating a Chicago Southside drug lord into confession, but also liberating him of his cold cash and stash. It looked like I was on the road to early retirement, if not perdition; too old and dishonorable for a City of Chicago Police Department pension, and too young for Social Security. With no money in the bank to speak of, my only trump card was an office apartment on Humphrey Avenue in Oak Park, and the resolution of the Danhurst case. When Internal Affairs placed me on administrative leave without pay, two weeks before I was summarily dismissed from the force, I finally put things into perspective, and made that same first trip that you had made years earlier to Edward Stawson's lair."

Those words, "Edward Stawson." It was as if lightning coursed through his veins at that precise moment, as he now gave Marbry his full and undivided attention. "Go ahead, Marbry, I'm all ears."

Marbry detected that Alex would be missing that first flight, after all.

"When I met Edward Stawson that morning," Marbry went on, "he appeared to be a likeable old gentleman. I couldn't put my finger on it, however, but something felt wrong. There was a 'strangeness' in the air. That is the only way I can explain it. From the moment I stepped into his office, apartment, clinic, or whatever you'd like to call it, I felt like I had been drugged. The air was heavy, and it was all so surreal, beginning with his nurse, Marie." At the sound of that name, Alex's eyes rolled back in his head. "So, I gather you know her, then."

Alex's mortuary nod said it all. "We've met. Go on, Marbry. Get it off your chest, and tell me why you're really here."

"When I asked Stawson if he knew you, he hesitated, and then stated that you were a patient of his who he hadn't seen in over four years. He said that was all he could tell me, but appeared more interested in me personally than you. He said I had the appearance of man worn down by life, and that he might be able to help me. I don't know how he did it, but he got me to open up, and tell him about my life, my failures, my job troubles, and my obsession with you and the Randy Danhurst case."

"My God, Marbry. How could you let that happen?" was Alex's exclamation, turned query.

"As you said earlier, Mr. Bales, leave God out of it. This is between you, me, and Stawson now. Like you, I gather, he promised me the moon and the stars, and, when I started taking his 'FOY2,' I became no better than you."

"FOY2?" Alex's jaw dropped. "Marbry, I know it's not in your nature, but you're going to have to trust me. You're in over your head. Where do you think I've been for the last six-plus years?"

"Stawson told me all about your FOY1 debacle."

"He did? Debacle? Is that what he called it?"

"You bet. He also confided that FOY2 was a much better product than the FOY1 aliquot. He said that he had now corrected all the 'downsides' of FOY1, and that FOY2 was the culmination of all his research, and his proudest moment. I don't know how I let him talk me into it, but, four years later, and a life below rock-bottom, I am still suffering the negative effects of FOY2. I thought you might be the one to help me, and remove the veil from my eyes. Honestly, I don't know where the last four years have gone, and I feel like I'm imploding from within. That's why I'm really here. Damn Danhurst. Damn you. It's Stawson I want. How many more souls is he going to take down before the Creator prevails?"

"There is no Creator, Marbry. Just Stawson and the infinite abyss. You fell for his sell, just like me, and I'll bet you're aging as fast as I am." Alex held up his right hand to show Marbry a dorsum riddled with venous highways more fitting for a Model T's cruise control than a high-performance Ford Shelby GT500.

"An anonymous phone call two weeks ago brought me here, Mr. Bales, and you're coming with me. We're going to put an end to this, one way or another."

"Correction, Marbry. I'm going it alone. You were just along for the ride. Don't follow me. You're just the ball-boy, and I'm the clean-up hitter. If you're good, I'll throw you a bone, but I'm the one who's gonna end this thing. Then we'll talk about Randy Danhurst. ¿Comprendes, Amigo? Are we clear on this?"

"Crystal. But sooner or later you're going to need my help."

"Not in this life, Marbry. Not in this life. Now, if you'll excuse me, I'll pack the few things I have in this hell-hole and be off. Like I said before, don't follow me. Now, get the hell out of here."

With little choice left, Marbry sheathed his 9mm "equalizer," and with no further words, gestures, or looks back forthcoming, made his way through the door, which had been left ajar during the entire verbal exchange. Alex had won Round One, but the bell for Round Two would most likely be rung shortly, and he couldn't shake the idea, the creeping suspicion, and his gut feeling that someone or something had been eavesdropping on his conversation with Marbry.

Unknown obstacles lay on the road ahead. Of that, he could be most certain. Alex, down for the count but not out, was like a pigeon with a broken leg. He was still able to fly, but his landing would be in doubt. Of little consequence would be air turbulence, as what would come after landing posed greater anxiety and trepidation than a fall from boundless heights. Fleeting premonitions bombarded ceaseless minutes, as a throwing of finite possessions into a creased leather bag and a terse call for a cab to the airport were clutched as tethers to his incessant flight of ideas. Where was this all going? Where would this all end? Alex was beyond a finger on a trigger and a barrel to the temple. He now had to see this thing through to the end, if not for curiosity's sake only. Proactive final arrangements could come later, after satisfaction or dissatisfaction brought the dead cat back. For some strange reason, his fragile state of mind rekindled a fun fact or totally worthless piece of information acquired during a college history class many moons before. At that time, Alex had imagined himself severely wounded at Gettysburg, during an American history lecture, and left at the mercy of a hundred and six Union physicians whose job it was to treat the scores and scores of Union and rebel wounded. There had been one small problem, however; that being that only thirty-five of the hundred and six were qualified to operate. Such utter anxiety and fear. Could it be that Stawson was a modern-day version of one of the thirty-five, or could he be considered just one of the majority of seventy-one going through the motions? Only time would tell, and there was not much of that left.

The jet arched northeastward to a Chicago showdown. In his window seat in first class, Alex gave the outward impression of a competent businessman fully in control of mind, matter, and destiny. Nothing could have been further from the truth, however, as the blank notepad and motionless fountain pen lay dormant on his tray table, and a brief glance out the window from time to time bred reenactment of the imaginary sensation of freefall through puffy, pillow-like, cumulus clouds in the rapid descent to what God only knew lay below. A game plan would have to be formulated now, and in short order, before arrival at O'Hare International Airport. Tarmac touchdown would preclude further strategy and catalyze implementation. Alex had to be prepared for any contingency, and a readiness manifested by hairs standing on end reminded him of bygone times when he was as competitive as the next man in the marketplace and on the world scene.

He would give it a run through step-by-step in his mind, if for no other reason than to ensure that his last stand went without a glitch. His apartment would be dusty, to say the least, after all these years, but everything would be in its proper place, especially the cold steel in a dresser drawer; now to be used for either protection or aggression, rather than self-determination. Alex would rest for a day or two, in order to muster his physical and mental resources, and then set out on the same elevated train route from downtown Chicago to Oak Park suburb to face an adversary, once thought friend, in his den of inequity. The "good" doctor, in a manner of speaking, was certain to be there, and they had so much to catch up on. Alex would hold the concealed pistol in his left trouser pocket, close to his thigh, just in case friendly chitchat turned into mortal discourse.

He knew not what he was up against, the natural or the supernatural. He knew not how he or his nemesis would react to one another, when hard, cold eyes met and formalities and niceties went out the window. What Alex did know was that Dr. Stawson had deceived him, had lied to him, and had in-volved him in an otherworldly game of cat and mouse, with the ultimate prize being eternal damnation in exchange for a transitory fountain of youth. That was far too high a price to pay for cosmetic conscientiousness and a shot of fictitious immortality. Fictitious, yes, because telltale signs of a return to the aging process had begun to reappear over the last six months. Were that not enough, he had been blindsided by Marbry, who had come out of nowhere, and reinforced his building hatred for the being on Humphrey Avenue. There was much, much more to this puzzle than had originally met the eye, and Alex was growing more and more impatient for resolution and vindication.

The honeymoon was over, and bittersweet reality had continued to set in. Morning aches and pains had for some time now become Alex's constant companions. At first, he thought them figments of his fertile hypochondriac's imagination, but, when creases and ever-so-slight wrinkles began to crisscross his now-hardened countenance, when facial and scalp hair began to tinge of salt and pepper, when sagging upper arm skin began to defy gravity, and when libido ran for the hills at the sight of swinging hips and a short skirt, he came to the long overdue and startling realization that his days were, indeed, numbered. Why had Stawson lied not only to him, but also to Marbry and God only knew how many others? What was to be gained from such a charade?

The crow's feet at the angles of his eyes in a bathroom mirror set his wheels in motion for the inevitable second installment and conclusion of the Stawson subjugation. The dogs of war would be unleashed in a day or two, bringing final resolution to pupil, mentor, or both. While dust had settled on the sheets covering dormant and aging furniture long ago relegated to the glue factory, Alex's overactive nervous system rehearsed an unchoreographed chain of events that would ultimately culminate in either a damming of source waters or a reinfusion of FOY1 and perhaps, now, FOY2's lifeblood.

Wrinkles, cracks, crevices, sciatica, low back pain, hair loss, chronic fatigue, and plain old inability to "get it up," damn the vacuum pumps, pills, paraphernalia, and oral stimulation, tolled the eleventh hour. With neither a hero's calm nor a coward's resolve to survive, he would draw a line in Oak Park's sand, and make a last stand fitting for an unhappy man of his stature. That last thought brought a smirk to a visage scarred by years and years of just getting by. His life had caused a great deal of unhappiness, especially to Marilina, and, now, at final act, he was about to be repaid in kind, with malice of forethought precluding peaceful resolution of the eventual conflict. The good doctor would be a fearsome adversary, and the element of surprise would most certainly not be in Alex's corner. In fact, Kalli, the warrior goddess, had most assuredly warned Stawson of Alex's second coming. Scratch subterfuge to counter superior numbers.

While fear has often been rationalized as a sign of intelligence, goading reflective examination of involved risks and possible consequences, anger, its child, has lurked in the wings; ready to spring with no advanced notice or warning when an ignorant countermove is the plat du jour. Make no bones about it, Alex was angry, and, yes, vengeance would be his, whether in this life or in the embers of lost souls, where two lifetimes of acquired understanding would serve him in good stead, as he counted the number of the Stawson beast. The Book of Revelations, Chapter 13, Verse 18, would have nothing on him, as he prepared to behold the number of a man, that Stawson "man" or whatever the hell he was, and that number would most certainly be six hundred three score and six. Science fiction? Supernatural hocus-pocus? Religious nonsense, fervor, or fanaticism? Maybe none, maybe all, or maybe some combination of the above. But who was to stop a runaway freight train or delusional express, namely Alex, from expressing his thoughts a mile a minute?

A little over forty-eight hours later, on what was to be the last day of second life, as he had known it, Alex awoke up at six a.m., as refreshed as he had ever been or could ever remember. The anticipation of resolution, catharsis, and/or vindication for the "cruel and unusual" that had been meted out to him by Dr. "Dubious," aka Edward Stawson, and his partners in crime had him bristling and biting at the bit. In Alex's mind, if Nuremberg were to be revisited, Stawson & Company would provide good company to bin Laden, Chavez, Gheddafi, Stalin, Castro, Hussein, Teppes, and a host of other famous, infamous, or posthumous tyrants. No sense pondering that now. It was time for action.

A brief shower, a light breakfast of oatmeal, instant coffee, and orange juice to dull hunger pains and unclutter wits, and a slip into his Sunday best were the immediate tasks before him. He relished the ordinary, as he prepared for the extraordinary. As Alex laced and tied his new wing-tipped shoes with an alacrity and meticulousness bordering on a high-tech surgical procedure, he recalled a verbal exchange of his first life, when his late, and only true, friend, Randy Danhurst, had playfully ribbed him to get his goat, early in their relationship. At that time, seated in living quarters that in no way were demonstrative of his hopes, aspirations, status in life, or future rise to stardom, business success, and subsequent riches, and in preparation for a double date with a pair of "honeys" who would raise temperatures, among other things, Alex was accosted by Randy on a lark. His concentration had been turned to his best white shirt, on which daily wear and tear had inflicted an unsightly gash at the right elbow sleeve, and just when he needed that indument most. Alex, the tailor, was not wasted on Randy.

"Where did you learn how to sew like that?"

"Here and there."

"Did you study medicine?"

"Would I be sewing my own damn shirt and chewing the fat with the likes of you, if I had studied medicine?"

"Too bad. You would have made a great surgeon."

Fast forward to the present.

"Great surgeon," yeah, but a surgeon gives life. As he descended to street level in the elevator, the bulge in Alex's left trouser pocket in no way indicated anticipated joy in an upcoming visit with his old friend or nemesis, but, rather, the blue steel that would most likely extinguish earthly, if not otherworldly, life.

The elevated train ride to Oak Park suburbia was uneventful. The tenements and burned-out buildings at and below rail level foreshadowed the no-holds-barred duel to the finish that would follow shortly. Alex, in his revisiting of Sherman's march to the sea, would leave nothing recognizable or useful in his wake, for either posterity or police department. Stawson, on the other hand, had, had more than enough time to fortify his office stronghold and post the once and again formidable gatekeeper, Marie Comanescu, a descendant of Third Reich womanhood who would have made der Führer proud even in those last bunker days.

This was not going to be easy. There would be resolution, however, once and for all. In a matter of hours, it would be all over. Funny how calm Alex was at that thought. Rest In Peace (RIP), closet skeletons. RIP, unfulfilled ambitions and failure to live up to expectations. RIP, any hope of Divine Deliverance or a seat at the Right Hand. Bite the bullet and go down like a man would be Alex's final testament and legacy to posterity, taking Stawson out, of course, in the process. The fires of hell were burning brightly, as Alex left the train behind and proceeded down the once glorious Lake Street to Humphrey Avenue.

Many moons past, street-smart thugs had extorted spare change from a desperate old man who had sought salvation to the tune of a newspaper ad. Not so, now. Time had invested Alex with further wisdom, and the taut, dry skin of his face, together with the sagging neckline and the pain in all his bones, were constant reminders that no shit would be taken this time around. He was a man on a mission, with nothing to lose, and projectiles would fly in any number of directions, before the din of small-talk, threat, or subtle coercion ceased. A 9mm round can do considerable damage at close range, and, while Alex in other circumstances might have been loathe to put it to the test, he knew all too well that forces beyond human control demanded discharge of his duty via his long-lost Italian accomplice, Beretta.

He took a right on Humphrey Avenue, and saw the apartment building in the distance. Half a block to go now. Fifty yards. He was there. It was too late to turn back now, and, besides, he had most likely already been spotted from above, as Stawson and staff prepared a welcome that would more than hold a candle to Odysseus' bachelor party.

He was in the vestibule of the building, pushing a button. No response came from the intercom, only white noise and static that promised no peaceful conclusion, and indicated a tendency toward restlessness of the natives. Then, a buzzer, and the door to the inner sanctum of offices lay open, for better and more likely worse. Bowels were laid bare, and transit to Stawson's lair became tantamount to a peristaltic wave, progressing in a single direction with no reverse flow; and with time enough only for brief sideward glances, and perhaps a paranoid cervical twist or two over the shoulder to ready for a possible rear action.

It was suddenly in front of him, that door. Years, seven of them, to be exact, had gone by, and, yet, that massive and immutable, wooden gateway to a world whose beings bordered on the crepuscular and surreal, had not aged, except for a handful of telltale scratches, cracks, and other signs of normal wear and tear common to thresholds of man or gates of hell. Thrown open with little regard for civil niceties or customary etiquette, the doorway revealed the blood-red scowl of eyes and countenance of Stawson's female stormtrooper, Marie Comanescu. She had not aged a bit, after all those years, and there was something truly hideous and unnerving about the posture and body language of welcome she had assumed. It was threatening and predatory, and took Alex by surprise, even in his "ready for anything," pregame strategy. She had come full circle since that candlelight amplexus in the Oak Park Arms Hotel seven years before.

"He's waiting for you."

An unnatural move of this gargantuan spider toward him, brought a reflex move of the fly to his trouser pocket and beyond, as he leveled firepower to her forehead.

"Back off, bitch."

"Calm down, Mr. Bales, you shall have your answers. Remember, it was you who found us. No one twisted your arm. We were only there to help. And you didn't seem to mind, that night we spent together in the Oak Park Arms Hotel."

Strange. She spoke as if she had been a major player, instead of one of the many puppets that "Geppetto" Stawson manipulated on the world stage.

"Where is he?"

"Through the doors. He'll see you now."

There appeared to be no one in the waiting or anterooms.

"Gimme your keys. Out the door."

He closed, locked, and barred further intrusion. With that powerful vixen out of sight and mind, Alex could concentrate on the work at hand. He would extract the information he required from that devil Stawson, and then end his earthly life, joining and accompanying him afterwards on the road to perdition and eternal damnation, for two lives spent cursing the Almighty and His gift of life. Blaspheming the latter and selling his soul for a second chance at life had been his curse and his condemnation. But wait a minute. Perhaps he was jumping to conclusions, and had gotten it all wrong. He had as yet to confront the being through the double doors. Had FOY1 been Alex's first unholy communion, or was he simply the result of a scientific experiment gone horribly wrong? Perhaps Dr. Frankenstein had been nothing other, and nothing more, than a scientific investigator with a penchant for bright ideas and dull outcomes. Perhaps the lackluster scientific result obtained had bordered on normal human error and acceptable statistical shortfall. Perhaps there had been no hocus-pocus involved, nor hand of the supernatural. Perhaps he had even contributed to medical science, in the form of the much improved FOY2. Joe Marbry, however, might have something to say on that score.

Alex made his way through the doors of final destiny. What he saw next brought shivers to his spine, raised hairs on both arms, and caused him to nearly lose his grip on and drop his pistol, which now appeared to be totally useless. There, before him, seated at his large oak desk and looking like a young man of no more than thirty-five years, was Edward Stawson. How could this be? What forces of heaven, hell, or Mother Nature had Stawson conjured up or called upon to aid in his outward transformation?

"Surprised, my boy?"

"It's been a long time, Stawson, and it's high time for some payback."

"Before you aim and discharge that inefficacious firearm, don't you want to at least satisfy your curiosity?"

"What for? We both know full well where this is going, and how it has to end."

"You nonetheless came here for explanations, and you shall have them. So, put that damn thing down, at least for a moment. You can use it later, if you see fit, on the one, the other, or both of us. I can assure you, however, that in my regard it will make little difference."

"What does that mean?"

"Just sit back and enjoy the yarn. Poe did, back in eighteen thirty, when our talk prompted a poem about loneliness and solitude, which he titled, Alone. Instead of taking his own life, he took comfort in my words. You could say I made him what he was. My price? Not his soul. Everything but. I exacted a toll on his earthly conscience far hotter and more unbearable than any fire and brimstone. That made me happy and him famous."

"Wait a minute. Who are you?"

"I'm sure you know by now. You've always known. You mean to tell me you fell for my FOY1 charade? Weren't you a little too big to believe in the tooth fairy, Santa Claus, or a fountain of youth? Even He would have grinned at your folly. To think, a second lease on life. That's rich. No mortal gets one. I who have lived many, and miserably, delight at your fall from grace. He has treated you no better than a creature of bad habit, like me, with one difference. While you will die and end up, I think you know where, I am condemned to heartlessly pawn off my wares on still another depressed, unsatisfied, or unrealized soul, like yourself. Rest assured, there will always be a new formulation of FOY1, and someone as rock-bottomed as you to test its waters. Didn't I find a down-on-his-luck cop to try my FOY2. Did you honestly believe that a mythical liquid could lift the veil of self-condemnation, or restore resilience to a body politic that long ago hemorrhaged every manner of hormone, neurotransmitter, circulatory lubricant, or nutritive matrix?"

"So, you're..."

"Never mind who I am. It's time."

Alex knew full well what those words meant, but, strangely enough, he felt no fear. Resolution was at hand, and he would not go down, literally or figuratively, without a fight. Perhaps he had been born for just such a day. Perhaps redemption for a life ill-spent hinged upon sending the beast crawling to a place from whence FOY1 and its successors might never again reemerge, except in its evaporative form. The price for failure was of no account, as Alex's trajectory had been only one way, since that fateful morning when he had spied a newspaper ad.

"You were always there, Stawson, Beelzebub, Mephisto, or whatever name you go by now. I sensed it. Chicago, Rome, San Francisco, the place mattered not. You would've followed me to the ends of the earth and time, and back, if only to have your pound of flesh."

Prayers would not come to him, as he lunged for Stawson's throat. Alex had been a lifetime sinner, and, in his hands, rosary beads would have been about as effective as juju beads against his nemesis from below or wherever. As his hands grasped air, his eyes caught sight of Marilina's visage, there, in front of him, and then that of Kalli. He had treated both badly, deservedly or not, and comeuppance was a bitch. As Alex blinked, to better focus on an adversary whose mirror image now stood directly behind him, the only card left to be played by a broken man in this life, this time, and this place of his death was flipped. As he spun and fired, an old ode he had once written to his end of days, titled Back to the Source, reverberated in his mind after exhumation from a cerebral gravesite; no less profound than its physical counterpart that would be readied by uncaring, unfamiliar attendants to house his limp body. The words now came matter-of-factly to his passive mind. There was no longer any sense of urgency.

Back to the source,
What does it seem,
Years of frustration,
Now but a dream.

Time better spent,
On good friends and love,
Cast to the wind,
When push came to shove.

Foolish in youth,
Foolhardy at play,
All things that mattered,
Became lost in the fray.

Whispers, like daggers,
Eyes in cold stare,
Colic and dander,
Too much to bear.

Chinks in the armor,
Baptized in the Styx,
Only figments of weakness,
As age exhumed old tricks.

Honors compiled,
Lecherous thighs,
Meted comeuppance,
Righted material lies.

One who has sinned,
One who was crowned,
Recollections meander,
Pyres sprout from the ground.

Back to the source,
What does it seem,
The river that roared,
Now damned to a stream.

***

"Wake up, Alex, wake up. Hang in there, buddy."

That voice was strangely familiar, from another time and place. Could it be? That was impossible. The cold tiles of a hard bathroom floor on his dorsum and the pinpoint glare and oscillations of the small luminescent orb on a stick were slowly, but surely, bringing Alex back to reality, from exotic destinations and a voyage that had perhaps circumvented only the globe of the mind. The red stickiness that had collected at the gashes in his wrists was a grim reminder of his return ticket. As he suddenly opened his shut eyes wide, a lost friend's face became painfully and joyfully evident.

"I thought we had lost you, brother. But you're back, and everything's gonna be okay. Why? Why?"

As paramedics worked frantically to fully resuscitate heart and lungs and stem the ebb and flow of Alex's lifeblood from vessels to ceramic pavement, he himself took solace and comfort in the gentle eyes and sober, solemn countenance of his friend Randy. Where had all the years gone? Had a lifetime transpired in a brief coma's hour? As the emergency medical technicians and paramedics shook their heads to the tune of teardrops on Randy's shirtfront, Alex drifted away from the light, if not from sound.

"I'm not going to leave you, Alex. I'm here for the long haul. I'll never abandon you again. These gentlemen are going to take you down to the ambulance now, and we'll get you fixed up and squared away at the hospital."

As he lapsed into unconsciousness, to be borne on wings hovering in the shades of gray between the world of pain and sorrow and the great beyond, Alex Bales confused out-of-body experience with flight of fancy. The jerk of the elevator's arrival at ground floor, followed within minutes by the thud of the ambulance's rear doors sealing his contents within, jolted momentary resurrection from the sepulcher of dreams. For better or worse, it had been a good life. A good two lives. His lives. From his supine position in reverse Trendelenburg, deep in the ambulance's bowels, Alex looked up to see Stawson at the wheel, putting the vehicle in gear. That was bad enough. When his glance, however, met that of the individual on the passenger side, his EKG flatlined.

Epitaph or Just the Beginning?

Season's Reason

Although I see the overcast sky above,
And dream of sunshine's light in distant lands,
Forever this earth will be my love,
As oceans hold no candles to desert sands.

Lives change in an instant as autumn leaves,
A blink of eye missing what does not suit,
Then winter sleep freezes what mother conceives,
And spring's sweet showers bring forth fertile fruit.

So, take what is given with no remorse,
When nature beckons to concede its gifts,
And follow life's journey back to the source,
Barring no pathways while healing all rifts.

For let it be said that no one is brave,
Who fools with season as if it were slave.

CPSIA information can be obtained at www.ICGtesting.com
Printed in the USA
BVOW08s2205120815

413159BV00003B/71/P